About the Author

As I grow older, details from earlier in my life are becoming more vivid than recent events. The other day, I had a flash of a cotton dress I wore sixty years ago. I felt the fabric, saw the faded circus pattern printed along the hem.

It came from The Clothes Exchange where greatcoats, worn shoes, woollen socks, horrible long-johns and occasionally a child's frock were laid out on trestle tables. After World War Two, everything – bread, butter, paper, meat, clothing – was in short supply.

As children, we didn't feel hard-done-by for we hadn't known any other time. And we were never properly starving. The Canadians sent us food parcels. Our grandmother sent us eggs.

I am now a granny myself. One of my grandsons asked me, 'Is it really true, Granny, you didn't have a fridge when you were little? Is it true there wasn't a telephone? Is it true you fetched your milk in a jug from the cow?'

Yes. All historically accurate. However, memory plays tricks. And so do writers. Not all the people in this story are the same as the people in my life.

Look out for other titles in the Moving Times *trilogy*

Bloom of Youth
Stronger than Mountains

Also by Rachel Anderson

Blackthorn, Whitethorn
The Flight of the Emu
Pizza on Saturday
Red Moon

Other titles published by Hodder Children's Books

The Glittering Eye
Cherry Heaven
The Diary of Pelly D
L.J. Adlington

The Carbon Diaries 2015
Saci Lloyd

Grandmother's Footsteps

RACHEL ANDERSON

Hodder
Children's
Books

A division of Hachette Children's Books

A Catalogue record for this book is available
from the British Library

ISBN 978 0 340 98159 7

Typeset in Bembo by Avon DataSet Ltd,
Bidford-on-Avon, Warwickshire

Printed and bound in Great Britain by
CPI Bookmarque, Croydon

The paper and board used in this paperback by Hodder
Children's Books are natural recyclable products made from
wood grown in sustainable forests. The manufacturing
processes conform to the environmental regulations of
the country of origin.

Hodder Children's Books
a division of Hachette Children's Books
338 Euston Road, London NW1 3BH
An Hachette UK company
www.hachette.co.uk

Contents

LITTLE GIRLS

ONE

The Day the World Ended for Ever

It was such a fine day when my entire world began to fall apart. I woke, that May morning, secure in the saggy camp-bed in my mother's mother's dressing-room.

'Hello Granny!' I called. 'Can we get up yet?'

The smell of generations of children's wettings wafted from the lumpy mattress beneath me. It was familiar, reassuring. I saw, through the gap in the wooden shutters, how the sky beyond was filled with happy clouds bobbing about in the blue like barrage balloons. I heard the contented cockerel crowing from the ridge of the hen-house like an all-clear siren. I watched the cawing rooks circle above their rookery in the beech trees like tiny spitfires clearing the sky of intruders. I knew all was well.

'Splendid! Barometer's going up! They said it would. Maybe we shall go bluebelling later on.' I heard my grandmother's cheerful weather-forecast greeting before the creak of her corsets as she lowered herself to the floorboards and began the quiet murmur of her morning prayer.

Every weekday, she knelt by her bed and asked that God's grace and loving kindness might fall upon all victims of suffering, especially the grieving, lonely women in faraway Germany whose husbands, brothers or fiancés were incarcerated behind wire fences in the Nissen huts on the edge of our village. Next, she thanked the Lord for safely bringing her to the beginning of this day, requested Him to defend her from falling into sin or from running into danger, and asked for His help that she might become righteous.

I was certain she was already very righteous. How could she want to be more so? She was perfectly good, even down to the pink strength of her corsets and the brightness of her china teeth in the flowery dish on the wash-stand.

Although she didn't mention me by name, I understood myself to be generally included in her messages to God. And since she was so regular in her prayers, they would most surely be noted.

So far, so good. Everything as it should be. God and Granny both watching out for me.

But then, round about elevenses time, the bad times began. I noticed how all the adults were becoming mad as hatters, rushing about doing unusual things. My grandfather was not tucked tidily away behind the roll-top desk in his study, writing sacred verses, surrounded by his caged canaries, his concordances and other holy books. Instead, he'd flung open both double doors at the front of the house. He was standing on the top step with outstretched arms, singing Hosannas at the chestnut trees.

Nor was Harold, the elderly outdoor handyman, calmly seeing to the polishing of the boots and the filling of the paraffin lamps in the outhouse, but was leaning on the scullery windowsill grinning at Meg, the indoor servant. She was not scouring the greasy pans with sand, but was leaning halfway out of the scullery window gawping up at the busy sky as though searching for a sign.

'I can't believe it! As I live and breathe, I just cannot!' she said, before her lower lip dropped down again and she continued her upward gaze.

My older cousins were not where they usually were, in the school room playing quiet morning games, but were whooping it up in the dining room, dancing round the polished table. I heard Cousin Kite, named after the bird of prey rather than a flying paper toy, say to his brother Cormorant something that sounded dangerously like: 'So let's see if we can get hold of some explosives first, shall we?'

'Righto.'

'Then we'll have a shot at making that Silver Cloudburst.'

Cousin Cormorant said, 'We'll have to snitch a cartridge from the gun-room and empty it out.'

I wasn't entirely sure what a Silver Cloudburst might be but I knew perfectly well that a cartridge was a brown cardboard tube, filled with lead pellets and gunpowder which had to be slipped inside a shot-gun before you could start killing things.

There were other big children, aside from the boy cousins, all older than me, who were also making the most of the adults' inattention. These were the disruptive strangers who stayed for short periods, with their sad jittery families, in the attic rooms at the top of the house because they'd got no homes of their own. Before the war, when there used to be live-in servants, the maids slept up here and had to creep down the back stairs so they wouldn't disturb the rest of the household.

At least, that's what my grandmother told me. 'And now, with the help of our Lord, we've all become accustomed to different ways of doing things.'

Today, the homeless children weren't keeping to their quarters. They were clattering up and down the the narrow carpetless stairs, then the wide carpeted front stairs, and all over, even right into Granny's glass conservatory to sniff at the delicate blue blossoms of her scented plumbago.

'Blimey, what a pong!'

'Yeah, but int it topping!' the scariest of them yelled as he raced back up to the landing and skimmed down the curving bannister rail. Even cousins Cormorant and Kite weren't supposed to slide down the banisters. Granny said it was most terribly dangerous. 'Silly boys. Supposing they lost their balance?'

But Cousin Cormorant said his mother had done it loads of times when she was young. The worst that could happen is you'd tumble on to Grandfather's Chinese gong in the hall. 'Then you'd make the most spiffing din.'

No, I thought. This chaos was neither spiffing nor topping. It was all most unsettling, and I hoped it would soon be over.

Then, amidst the confusion, my own lovely, fluffy, curly-headed mother disappeared. One moment there she was kneeling on the ground in front of me, hastily buttoning my shoes (which had been polished to a bright chestnut shine like a ripe conker by Harold before he took to grinning like an imbecile). And she'd been grumbling, 'When *will* you learn to do them up for yourself? I'm sure Mary knew how by your age.'

The next moment, suddenly she was nowhere. Gone. Whoof! Like a silent explosion. Not here looking after me, not anywhere. Gone away without an explanation or a goodbye peck on the cheek.

How could she do this to me? Disappearing was the sort of thing that happened to my father, not to her.

'M-u-u-u-m! Where are you?'

So then I too began to scurry this way and that, just like the rest of them, only less happily, along the creaking landings and down the shadowy passages, before shooting as fast as a lead pellet out of the side door beside the water pump. I scattered the hens gathering like refugees for their tablecloth crumbs. I ran on without stopping, desperate to escape the madness. I paused to glance back and check if she was at any of the windows looking out. She wasn't. Instead, to my horror, I noticed how the evacuee who'd been sliding down the banisters was now right up on the roof. He'd climbed out through an attic sky-light. He was tying a bed-sheet to the lightning conductor. On the sheet he'd written some words in dribbling letters. It looked like stove-blacking rather than paint.

The boy was crazy. What if he slipped and fell?

The breeze flapped his banner. It unfurled. I could see his message.

GOD SAVE THE KIND! it said.

I couldn't bear to wait for the moment when he fell to earth. I stumbled on till I found myself in a dank place beneath the yew trees. I'd lost any sense of direction. I couldn't work out how I'd got here, let alone how to find the way back. Yews were said to be full of magic. The twisted yew trunks over in the churchyard contained the writhing souls of heathens who'd died unbaptised and unrepentant, or so Cousin Cormorant had warned me.

I waited, as you were supposed to during air-raids, trying to be patient and calm, hoping that Granny's prayer to deliver us from evil covered me too, even though I hadn't actually said the words. As for that boy's message, would God see it? And was I kind? Would God save me?

I did so need saving from loneliness, evil and fear.

I snivelled, but quietly. Nobody out there must hear, not those big rough cousins who laughed and would call me a soppy cissy, and specially not that wicked man, Hitler who'd been trying to kill us all since long before I was born.

TWO

Nuns in Boots

It was Hitler's fault that my sister and I were living here. It was supposed to be a haven of safety. Our grandfather was rector of the parish. Our grandmother was the rector's wife. This carried just as many responsibilities though they were not so apparent to the general eye. Because we were young, our mother was with us, or had been till this morning when she went missing without telling anyone. If you went Absent Without Leave in the army, it was called AWOL and you got court-martialled.

I thought that we'd probably been bombed out some time ago, but somehow that didn't make us homeless in the same way as it did the boy up on the roof.

'It's not very nice being called a homeless person,' Granny had said. 'Best not, if you can help it. A bit like the wandering tribes of Israel. Forty years before they found somewhere to lay their heads and settle their flocks.' She spoke fondly of them, as though they were distant relatives.

The rectory was surrounded by woods and farmland as

far as you could see. If you stood on tippy-toe on the wobbly stool in Granny's dressingroom, you could see all the way across the marshes to the misty blue of the South Coast. This was exactly where Hitler's armies would try to arrive for their invasion of Britain, but would become entangled in the coiled barbed wire on the beaches.

'Probably,' said Cousin Cormorant darkly. 'Though some of them might get through.'

Despite being deep in countryside, staying at the rectory was not unlike living at Victoria railway station, perpetually busy with the arrivals and departures of family and strangers, of evacuees, refugees, war widows, people mysteriously referred to as fallen women, brave service people on special leave, prisoners of war, called the POWs who came under escort to use Granny's piano or to play chess with our grandfather.

Beneath the dark heathen branches of the yews, time moved forward like a snail. It felt like hours later that I saw one of the many strangers passing quite near by. She had Granny's two bad-tempered Pekinese dogs yapping at her heels and she was carrying a bunch of sandy carrots in her arm. I thought for a moment that she must be one of the aunts. But she didn't have the halo of soft red curls and she wasn't being very kind to the dogs. The aunts were kind to all dogs, kinder than they were to children. This woman was trying to kick the dogs out of her way.

'Why d'you have to keep following me?' she snapped. I thought I even heard her call them 'beastly little bitches' which was quite wrong. Only Jonquil was a bitch. Polyanthus was definitely a dog, son of Jonquil.

Perhaps they recognised the smell of the woman for she was wearing one of my grandmother's hairy tweed suits, also a pair of her second-best lisle stockings (which the dogs were ruining), and her diamond brooch where it almost didn't show, tucked under the collar of the borrowed jacket. In fact, if the sunlight slanting through the trees hadn't caught the diamonds and set them afire, I wouldn't even have noticed them. My grandmother righteously lent precious things to all sorts of people who turned up having lost everything.

'One has to try to remember our Lord's parable of the good Samaritan,' she said. 'Even if sometimes one would rather not.'

The woman noticed me there against the tree.

'Why hello petkins,' she said, familiar even though we'd never met before. She thrust the carrots into my arms. The fluffy green foliage trailed like a magnificent bouquet. 'Your Nana asked me to fetch vegetables for the soup. I suppose she thinks I'm some kind of housemaid. And which one might you be? There's so many of you, I'm blowed if I can work out which belongs to who. You'll probably be one of Speranza's tribe?'

One of Aunt Speranza's children? Heaven protect me from that. Aunt Speranza had hefty boys with big boots who ran round the dining room table like tigers shouting about gunpowder. What a fate to have one of them for a brother.

'I'm Ruth,' I said.

'After your grandmother? So at least there's a few sensible names in this family.'

What did she mean? A name was a name. This was the first time I'd heard a hint that some of my relatives' names might be peculiar. I still hadn't understood the full complexity of Grandfather's system for naming his eight offspring. The uncles were Falcon, Merlin, Kestrel and Guillemot with sisters called Charité, Speranza, Thrift, and Veritas. Veritas was my mother. Her name, if translated from Latin, meant truth,

'What were you doing alone out the back here?' She glanced shiftily round. 'Didn't you know the world's ended?'

At least that's what I thought she said.

'You ought to be having a happy time with everybody else, not skulking round here. Now you run along. And take these brutes with you.'

'I got myself lost,' I sniffed.

'Looks like you're still all in one piece. You use your ears and listen carefully. You'll soon catch up with the others.'

Would I? Listening struck me as a daft way of looking for something. I didn't believe for a second it'd work. When adults listened, they mostly heard bad things, like planes going over low. Then, they went rigid.

'Ours or theirs?' they whispered.

They listened out for sirens too. When they heard them wailing, they grabbed hold of you and ran like wildfire. If they hadn't heard anything all day, then they gathered round the wireless set for the news and you had to keep quieter than a church mouse so they wouldn't miss anything.

The dog-hater cupped her hand round her ear. 'Over there,' she said and pointed through the impenetrable thicket of rhododendron bushes. 'Off you go now, and pretend you didn't see me.'

Perhaps the woman was spy. You never knew for sure when spies might not here in our midst.

'They'll parachute in, disguised as nuns,' Cousin Cormorant warned me. 'You'll be able to recognise who they are by their boots.'

When I believed him, he fell about laughing.

The babble of excited people was definitely coming from the front of the house. But why was everybody round there? The front was for formal visitors – the Air-Raid Protection officer when he came to complain about the blackout, the bishop when he came to complain about Grandfather's sermons, young men who needed an emergency marriage because they'd been posted overseas and their girl was in the family way, parishoners requiring burials, witnesses, or comfort when their loved ones were reported missing in action. But children round the front, never.

Yet here was the entire household, including Grandfather singing, all hanging about in scary chaos round the front door, as though expecting something important to happen.

If this was indeed the end of the world, it wasn't like the warnings in the Bible. No trumpets speaking, no archangels with their excesses of wings, no beasts with flashing eyes in front and behind. The trees and grass weren't burning up. Nor was it hailing with fire and blood.

Aunt Speranza was pulling a tangle of red, white and blue bunting out of a dusty cardboard box which had been stuffed at the back of the fancy-dress cupboard for as long as I could remember. My aunt was persuading old Amy to help drape the strings of flags along the laurel bushes. Amy wasn't very good at it. She wasn't very good at anything. Old Amy wasn't really old. But she was definitely as daft as a brush, or so I heard people whisper. Even with a screw loose, according to our grandmother, she was still a precious child of God and everybody had to be nice to her, whatever they thought of her privately.

'Well stripe me pink, Amy! Don't that look pretty as a picture,' said Meg the domestic cheerfully.

No one had ever done this sort of thing with flags before. It wasn't tidy and it wasn't safe. Coloured flags, even faded ones, would draw attention to our presence as clearly as that white sheet on the roof. The pilot of a spotter plane would be bound to notice. Perhaps even Hitler himself with his crazy swivelling eyes would see.

'No,' I said. 'It looks dangerous.' I searched out the majestic figure of my grandmother who luckily hadn't gone AWOL like my mother. I thrust the carrots at her.

'Ah there you are, my dear,' she said from her great height. She didn't pick me up. Just as well. She was wearing her dark green uniform suit for the Women's Royal Voluntary Service. The tweedy wool was so coarse it grazed your skin like sand-paper. She gave me her hand to hold, cool and papery like dry chestnut leaves. I clung on, avoiding the prickly cuff of the jacket.

'That's it, my dear, you stay close,' she said. She ignored my sniffs. 'And I see you've brought my two naughty dogs back too. Well done. Your mother's gone to see if there's a train. She wished to go up to town.'

'Town' meant London, a terrible place with doodlebugs droning through the sky, searchlights cutting through the dark.

'To look for your father. Though goodness knows if she'll ever find him. I should imagine the crowds will be dreadful, just like the Jubilee.'

So what would happen if my mother never found my father in the crowds? And got lost and never came back? I'd begun to forget what she looked like. I'd completely forgotten what my father looked like.

'Why, isn't that *splendid*?' Granny said to the younger women draping flags on bushes. 'Very gay! Like gypsy washing hung out to dry, wouldn't you say? So anyway, my dear, I gave Veritas some money for her ticket. She hadn't any. Though I don't suppose there'll be any trains running, not on a day like this. Never mind. She's bound to have fun. She usually does.'

'Cormorant's doing fireworks!' a boy's voice called.

'And there's going to be a gurt bonfire!' one of the others shouted. 'With a procession. And lighted flambeaux!'

Abandonment by my mother, domestic disorder, and any

moment, organised conflagration. What a terrible day.

Cousin Kite prattled excitedly on about his brother's Silver Cloudburst. As I clung to our grandmother's hand, my other hand was being tugged. It was Mary, trying to drag me away.

'Come *on!*' she hissed. 'Don't be a scaredy-cat. Don't you even want to *see*?'

What was there to see? Where was she going?

'You've *got* to come,' she insisted.

Curiosity won. After all, Mary knew about things. If she said to go, it had to be worthwhile.

THREE

Quick March, Best Feet Forward

'It's going to be wizard fun! We'll go right down to the end of the drive. We'll find out what's happening out there. We'll be like secret agents. We'll report back to the cousins.'

She knew we weren't allowed down the drive on our own.

'Today's different,' Mary said. 'They won't mind. They probably won't even notice. Not now the war's ended.' She wouldn't let go of my hand in case I changed my mind.

'The war?'

'Yes. Didn't anybody tell you?' Mary was two years older. Whatever was going on, she cottoned on faster then me. She could do loads of things I couldn't, even thump the boy cousins if they got out of hand. The only thing she couldn't do was read. Some of the grownups thought this was odd.

'Oh,' I said.

'Didn't you realise?'

I thought, So that's what all the fuss is about.

I'd felt bad about the end of the world. The end of the war was going to be much worse. The grownups were always going on about Before the War. What they'd done, the food they'd eaten, how late into the nights they'd danced. But I knew that Before The War was just a fairy-tale time. It had never really existed. There'd always been War. The war was life. Without it, there'd be nothing but an empty vacuum like a bomb crater. Whatever unknown substance came to fill it, was bound to be unsettling.

'Please hurry!' Mary urged. 'Or we'll miss the band.' It was a quarter of a mile to the five-barred gate at the end of the drive. 'There'll be soldiers parading and music playing and people cheering. And if we don't get there in time, we won't see any of it.'

She was behaving like our mother. Craving excitement. Veritas would run a mile just to catch up with a marching band or to watch a convoy of camouflaged lorries rumble by. I used to think it was because she hoped for a glimpse of our father.

'Don't be daft!' Mary had said. 'Father's not a *soldier*! He does something secret and important.'

What could be more important than fighting?

She was trotting us, not the direct way, but round the stable yard, along the side of the woodshed, past the dog-pens where Grandfather's vicious prize terriers raced noisily up and down. They must have envied the freedom they saw being enjoyed by our grandmother's lap-dogs.

The back-drive curved through the trees away from the house, before rejoining the main drive. It was used by the carrier's van, the water-cart, and servants in the days when they had to keep their comings and goings out of sight. Striding along ahead of us, we saw the dog-hater, wearing our grandmother's grey suit. She was carrying a suitcase. She was in a big hurry. Perhaps she wanted to watch the marching soldiers. She was soon out of sight.

At the end of the drive, Mary heaved me up on to the top of the five-barred gate for a better view of whatever there might be. The chalky white road stretched away, flat and deserted, towards the willow-hurdle-maker's cottage one way, and towards the hill that led up to St. Augustines's parish church the other. There was no traffic. No haycart, no stray dog, no herd of cows, and certainly no marching band. We waited until Mary got bored. No living creature passed by to celebrate the ending of the war.

'I expected a better turn-out than this!' Mary grumbled. She slid under the gate. Daringly, she strode into the middle of the lane. She held her arms out wide, like Grandfather when he was on the chancel steps giving the valedictory blessing to the congregation.

'Come back!' I shrieked. There was always so much to be afraid of. 'You'll get run over!'

'In a minute. I'm making the most of our new freedom from tyranny.' She must have heard that expression on the wireless. She'd never used it before.

We ambled back towards the house, dismayed by the lack of entertainment. Mary had another idea. 'I know! I'll find you a mole to cheer you up.'

'I don't want a mole.'

'Let's just rescue one anyway, as our good deed for the day.'

The field beside the drive was scattered with soft earthy mole-humps. The farmer didn't like them. He pushed traps into them. We found the metal top of one sticking out and dug deeper with our hands till we managed to pull it up. The victim was well past being rescued, squeezed to death round its plump velvet waist by the tight clasp.

'Some of our soldiers died in France like this,' Mary said.

'Yes, I know,' I said, though I had only the vaguest idea where France might be.

'This is worse than what Germans do,' Mary said grimly. As she released the body from the trap for decent re-burial, the hurdle-maker's wife came out of her cottage and began to yell across the field.

'You leave them traps be! You meddling wretches. I'll tell the rector on you! Deserve your backsides tanning. You and your brothers!' She must have meant Cormorant or Kite.

So we ran. We reached the house. I saw that the banner fluttering from the roof had been corrected from GOD SAVE THE KIND to GOD SAVE THE KING but this hadn't prevented the grownups from getting into a state of panic, though not because of the boy and his bad writing.

It was an insignificant matter for a skinny East End lad who'd been bombed out of his home to twice risk his neck slithering about on the roof-top, but was quite another matter for two of the reverend's granddaughters, along with a brooch set with diamonds, to disappear. Cousin Cormorant warned us that the aunts feared we'd fallen to the bottom of the drinking well. If not that, then slipped into the stinky cess-pit. Or gone to fish for tiddlers and drowned in the pond.

'And Granny thinks you and her diamonds have been stolen away by the gypsies,' Cousin Cormorant said with a laugh. 'Which you haven't, worse luck.'

The panicking grownups decided it was Mary's fault for leading me astray. I was too young to understand, they said.

'Mary's really for it,' Cormorant warned. 'Sounds like she'll be shot at dawn. Or beaten at least.'

Our grandmother's two dogs had been beaten when they ran across the marshes and chased the sheep.

'But we *didn't* run away,' I told Cormorant. 'Why should we want to? We like it here.'

'I don't care,' said Mary defiantly, sticking out her jaw as she was led upstairs to our grandmother's bedroom. She didn't struggle, even though Granny was holding her very firmly by the arm. She just stuck out her lower lip even further.

When Polyanthus and Jonquil were punished for

harrying the lambing ewes, it was with a riding crop. They howled and hung their heads with shame. Mary had wailed on the dogs' behalf, that it wasn't fair, that the poor litle Pekes couldn't understand. But both grandparents believed in the moral responsibility of all God's creatures. Certainly, Jonq and Pol never chased after sheep again, though they continued to chase hens, tease prize terriers in pens, and nip children's ankles.

So what would Mary be beaten with?

'Probably only a soppy old hairbrush,' Cousin Cormorant said knowingly. 'That's all you drippy girls can take. At our school, it's the strap.'

Which side of a hairbrush? The smooth black ebony side or the terrible bristly hedgehog side?

'Smooth of course,' said Cormorant with a grin which showed his missing tooth. He relished seeing us in trouble.

I expected to hear howls from under the door of Granny's bedroom. Nothing. I wondered if perhaps Granny was beating Mary only *very gently* with a comb? Cormorant laughed till I blushed with shame.

'A *comb*! You silly drip,' he said. 'What'd be the point in that?'

Much later, when we played on the swing, Mary told me, 'Course she wouldn't *really* do anything. Not even pretend. She loves us too much. She just said I ought to buck up my ideas a bit.'

'How?'

'Try harder to learn to read, try to be tidier, brush my

hair a hundred strokes every day. Then she gave me a barley sugar twist.'

'Barley sugar?' I said, impressed. We knew about sweeties from story books and gossip but we never saw any. Mary had told me that Veritas swapped our sweetie ration coupons with spivs for things that were more useful like gin, and stockings.

'It was ever such an *old* barley sugar. All soft, with bits of fluff on it. She's had it hidden in her drawer for years and years, probably since before the war. I've seen it there lots of times.'

But now it was After the War. A new way of life was about to start. And Granny's diamond brooch was still missing.

She came and found us by the swing. She had on her galoshes and her raffia gardening hat.

'Ah, there you are, girls!' The business of going down the drive was forgiven – for the time being anyhow. Granny had a wooden wheelbarrow and her small border fork. 'I'm afraid we can't go bluebelling this afternoon. I've got to dig for sardines.'

'Can we help?'

'I do wish you would, dears.'

Old Amy, who wasn't really old but was definitely daft, and Cousin Kite came too.

'Digging for victory!' sang Kite, leading Amy by the hand so she wouldn't get lost.

Only Granny knew where the sardines were buried. And

even she couldn't remember exactly.

'You should've made a map,' said Kite. 'Like with burying land-mines.'

We dug and we trudged, from behind the dog-runs in the back yard, to the base of the warm brick wall where the nectarines grew, back across the mossy lawn to a hidey-hole beneath the quince tree. There was a small *cache* in the shallow leaf-mould under the scary yew tree where I'd been so lost that morning. If only I'd known then that treasure lay right beneath my feet. It had been on Ministry advice, for use in the event of invasion. To foil the enemy, Granny explained, she'd never buried more than three tins in any one place.

'And now, I believe we're like the red squirrels,' she said. 'Searching for our hidden hazelnuts.'

'Squirrels, squirrels,' agreed Amy wagging her head up and down like the wooden bird at the top of the cuckoo clock. I'd once overheard Meg the maid whisper that Amy had a good deal more than just a few loose screws and she ought to be put away.

The cans, once a sunny yellow, were now so rusty that the sardine pictures hardly showed at all. The keys were gone too.

'Guess what's for our supper tonight?' Granny said with the smile of the smug squirrel.

Cold sardines lay in pairs on their slices of toast like twin corpses on a bier. The tiny bones poked through the silvery skin.

Poor dead fishes dug up from the quiet of their graves, I couldn't eat them because they looked so sad. But what one person left on her Bunnykins plate, a cousin named after a voracious sea-bird would eagerly gobble down.

'And clear plates mean clear consciences,' said Granny giving Cormorant a nod of approval.

FOUR

Peace in Our Times

In peacetime, which was still going on the following morning, the rooks spun more dizzily above the trees, the cock crowed more joyfully and the Germans, enemy prisoners no longer, were free to wander the lanes as they waited for repatriation, some of them falling in love with local girls like Meg and deciding not to return to the homeland after all.

But the business of Granny's diamonds was not yet done with.

'Such a shame,' she sighed meaningfully as she laced up her corsets. 'I thought they'd have turned up by now. My dear father gave them to me on my twelfth birthday.'

Twelfth? Could this fine ancient person, nearly as tall as a mountain, with dry knobbly knuckles like old wood, creaky joints like branches in the wind, and magnet grip on morality and history, ever have been a girl of twelve?

'Mother, are you *quite* sure it wasn't Vee who took them?'

Aunt Speranza dared to accuse her own absent sister of theft.

When they said 'Mother', I knew they meant Granny.

'We all know she never has two beans of her own. She's always borrowing.'

'Of course it wasn't. I gave her ten shillings to see her through,' said Granny, standing up to one daughter for another.

But the seed of doubt had been planted. If not Veritas, then perhaps her daughter?

After breakfast, Granny took me aside and looked at me, straight and serious, right into my eyes. Through the thick lenses of her spectacles, her own eyes seemed hugely round like goldfishes'. Short-sighted though she was, I knew she could see me very clearly. Probably, like God, right through me and into my soul.

'Ruth, I have to ask you something. And you must tell me the truth. You know what the truth is, don't you?'

'Yes.' It was one of the ten commandments that God gave to Moses written on a piece of stone which was a very difficult thing to do. Thou shalt not kill. Thou shalt not bow down to any graven image. Thou shalt not tell fibs.

'Ruth, yesterday, when we couldn't find you, where were you hiding?'

'With Mary, like she told you. She took me to look for the music.'

'Before then? When you disappeared?'

No, she'd got it wrong. *I* never disappeared. It was Veritas who'd disappeared, and still not reappeared.

'Did you come upstairs and borrow my diamonds, off the dressing table?'

Of course I hadn't. Yes, of course we admired Granny's pretty things, the silver-backed clothes brushes, the silver pin-box given to her by her mother, with the engraved inscription *Rejoice Evermore, Pray Without Ceasing*, the long sharp hat-pins, the staring, humourless wax dolls, and especially the diamonds. When not pinned to the lapel of her jacket, they were spiked into the velvet pin-cushion beneath the looking-glass so that you could see rainbows dancing round their edges just as I'd seen them dancing yesterday peeking slyly out from under the woman's collar. But *take* Granny's things? No, never, for thou shalt not steal, unless you were boy cousins who wanted to snitch gunpowder out of a cartridge.

I said, 'I think you lent them to one of the ladies who was staying.'

'Oh botheration the woman! It was my suit I lent her, not my brooch,' Granny said angrily, then immediately regained her temper. 'Never mind. I'm sure Cecilia had her reasons. She probably needs them far more than I do. And I can always make do with my old pearls, can't I?'

Her pearls were the colour of chips of broken tooth and didn't dance like diamonds. When I grew up, would I be as tolerant towards my trespassers?

Later, Granny explained it to the aunts. 'It's all right, the mystery's solved. Ruth actually saw Cecilia taking them.'

Not taking, just wearing, and hurrying off down the drive.

Cormorant snarled at me, 'You stupid little ninny! Now they're gone for ever. Poor Granny. If you saw, you should've *done* something. You should've snatched them back!'

'No she shouldn't!' Mary stood up for me more stoutly than our mother's sisters stood up for her. 'She's only young. The thief might have turned on her and knifed her to death.'

Aunt Speranza said she thought it strange that Cecilia, who was so nicely-spoken, so fond of dogs, and a distant relative of Bishop Sparrow's wife, should turn out to be a thief. But I knew differently, that Cecilia kicked dogs and disliked children. It was far stranger that the POWs, who were the evil enemy, had never stolen so much as a slice of bread on their visits to the rectory.

The aunts weren't satisfied. They grumbled on, turning their bitterness over and over like the rotting matter in Granny's compost heaps. The frequent separations from their husbands made them sour. I'd heard them talk before, how Veritas always had all the luck, how *her* husband wasn't even in uniform but in some hush-hush place in London so she'd been able to see him whenever she wanted.

'And always dumping you and Mary here!' Aunt Speranza turned on me. 'It's just not right, not fair on Mother and not fair on you.'

Aunt Thrift agreed. 'Vee's been so thoughtless. Mother

has quite enough to do without looking after Vee's girls as well.'

'But Granny likes having us,' I said. Because I'm her favourite, I almost added.

'It's too much for her at her age,' said Aunt Speranza.

'Veritas should be looking after you herself,' said Aunt Thrift.

'Or at least get in a nanny,' said Aunt Speranza. 'Besides, Vee always forgets your ration books. There's never enough food to go round.'

Even before we found the sardines, there seemed enough, specially if you liked porridge. There were also eggs from the hens. And vegetables from the kitchen garden. And rabbits from the woods. And milk from the farm. And pippins and pearmains from the apple loft (when the mice hadn't got to them first). And mulberries from the mulberry tree. And chestnuts from the chestnut trees.

Later, behind the grownups' backs, Cousin Cormorant said through narrowed eyes, 'And another thing. You're not even clean. I've seen your necks. You've got tide-marks. And your ears.'

Mary couldn't deny it. Although our mother and our Granny encouraged us to say our prayers and brush our hair, neither of them ever made us have a bath.

The rectory was not on the mains supply. For the kitchen, water was drawn from the pump. For the bathroom, it had to be hauled upstairs in buckets. Every morning before her prayers, our Granny performed a complicated process, which she called her *toilette*, standing at her marble wash-stand, when she washed herself discreetly all over from face to feet using a single ewerful of cold water. Mary and I wiped our faces once a week, more of a lick and a promise than a wash, after our boiled eggs and before Sunday Mattins.

'That's why you smell,' said Cormorant.

'No we don't.'

'You soon will. And then you'll rot away. And good riddance too.'

'We're more patriotic than you. We've been saving water,' Mary replied staunchly.

A poster on the village notice-board had urged everybody to fill their bath-tubs no deeper than five inches. Only half a dozen of the village houses even had a bathroom.

'And saving soap!' I added. Soap was on ration too.

'Dirt keeps us warm. So we've been saving coal too!' Mary triumphantly crowed at Cormorant. *Save Fuel to build more battleships* was another of the stirring propaganda posters. Uncle Kestrel was on a battleship somewhere in the Atlantic. So I felt certain that the poster was aimed directly at our family.

We ran after Granny to help in her latest search, for lost hen's eggs. In keeping with the new freedom, they'd been laying anywhere except in their coops. In flowerbeds, on the compost heap, under the laurel bushes.

'Ooh this is such fun!' said Granny. 'It reminds me of

those lovely egg-hunts we used to have Before The War.'

'What's an egg-hunt?' we asked.

'On Easter Day for the Sunday School children. We hid them all over the garden. They were made of chocolate of course.'

Cormorant claimed he could remember chocolate eggs. 'Wrapped in silver paper. All different colours.'

Eggs made of chocolate! 'What else did they make out of chocolate?' I asked and suggested chocolate flowers, clocks and motor cars.

'Chocolate *clocks*?' said Cormorant scornfully. 'Don't be stupid. Only eggs. Sometimes you're nearly as daft as Amy.'

Next morning, listening in on Granny's prayers, I heard the name 'Cecilia' joining the list of those in need of God's special blessing.

Would any of us, I wondered, ever become as old and as absolutely righteous as our grandmother?

'Course we won't,' said Mary.

'Not even if we prayed for every second of every minute of every day for the rest of our lives?'

'Shouldn't think so,' she said, with a hopeless shrug.

'Why not?'

'Because we're not parson's wives, are we? That's what makes her the way she is.'

'Closer to God?'

'Sort of. That's how she knows the rules.'

'What rules?' I only knew about the Commandments.

'About how to be good. You'd have to marry a churchy

parson to be like that. And you wouldn't want that, would you?'

I didn't know. It was too soon in life to have to start thinking about marriage.

'Even poor Granny didn't want to marry a curate,' said Mary. 'But she went and fell in love, didn't she?'

Did she? I supposed my sister must be right. She usually was.

All the same, I did so much want to follow in Granny's footsteps, not just in name, but in every detail, even down to the daily top-to-bottom *toilette* in cold water.

On the day the war ended, she'd told me to stick by her and I'd be all right. I was going to do just that, to stay as close as I could, for ever and ever.

But it wasn't to be. Already, just a week after the ending of the war, Veritas was making her excited way down Buckingham Palace Road towards Victoria railway station where she would get on the slow train that would carry her to Spellingly railway halt. There, she'd get off, and saunter the three miles along the footpath to return to her parents' home.

And in her new postwar mind, Veritas was already working on quite other plans for our future.

GROWING GIRLS

FIVE

London Life, City Strife

'At last!' she said. 'I've found us a simply marvellous new place to live! You'll both adore it! A thin house, on five floors. It's taken a bit of bomb damage so there's a hole in the roof, and no stairs at the moment. But we'll soon fix that when Granny agrees to lend us the money.'

I was so surprised to see her again, all pink-cheeked with excitement, with her frizzy red curls tied up in a brand new Victory head-scarf and a strange dress that looked as though she'd made it out of a Union Jack, that I hardly took in what she was actually telling us.

'We'll move in, and Father too, and have a new little baby and live happily ever after. Because now the war's over, everybody wants to have lots of babies and everything's going to be such a lark for us all!' Veritas liked things being larky, though her kind of fun was different from Granny's. More partying, less praying. I remembered her telling us one noisy night that even air-raids were fun because you always met new people down in the shelter, just like at a party. You just had to get yourself in the right mood to be awake all night.

'Babies?' said Mary making an I'm-going-to-be-sick face. 'What for?'

'For love. A dear brother for you to play with and help look after.'

'Not a brother. Babies is all right I suppose, but no boys,' said Mary firmly.

'Yes, no boys,' I echoed loyally.

'If you ever dare have any boy babies we'll throw them in the dustbin,' said Mary. 'And slam the lid down to squash them flat.'

But you could tell that Veritas was set on boy babies from the doting way she sometimes looked at her nephews, specially at young Puffin squawking and dribbling down the front of his blue knitted matinée jacket. Mary said she'd heard our mother ask Aunt Charité, who'd had five sons one after another, how she'd managed it.

Almost before we had time to say proper goodbyes to Jonq and Pol, or one last play with the Noah's Ark animals, Veritas whisked us away. And here we were, having to live where there were streets with drab stone pavements, and where, instead of fetching milk in a tin can from the farm, it was brought in glass bottles to your doorstep by a horse and cart.

'I don't like it,' I said. It was too different and there was no grass. Even the milk-horse didn't get any grass. In its nose-bag was nothing better than dry chopped chaff.

38

No wonder it slopped along so slowly.

'Of *course* you like it,' said Veritas cheerily. 'You were born within the sound of Bow Bells. So that makes you a Londoner. In fact, you're the only one of us who is a true Londoner.'

Also here in London was our father, grey and exhausted from six years doing secret things to help win the war. We hardly recognised him but somehow we'd have to get used to him. Veritas obviously adored him, in fact much preferred his company to ours. At least that's what Mary told me when she took me out to explore the bomb-sites.

'We're being kind to them, keeping out of their way,' she said.

In the rubbled basements of empty houses, we dug for treasure. We never found any, but we built castles from broken bricks, and created secret gardens amongst the purple flowering weeds which grew as tall as country foxgloves.

Whatever we were doing, I always felt hungry. Mary said, 'It's because you're growing.'

But it wasn't just that. It was also because Veritas didn't know how to cook and because food was scarce. Practically everything was still on ration. To be allowed to queue for grey sausages, grey bread, grey National Flour, and greasy grey mouse-trap cheese, you needed enough of the right coupons in your ration books. You also needed money, time, patience and organisational skill. Veritas was always swapping our coupons with rich neighbours for more important things like gin and stockings. It was illegal. She could've gone to prison for it. So could the neighbours.

At least Veritas had plenty of enthusiasm.

Mary and I were on one of our treasure-seeking expeditions when a small miracle happened which felt similar to the devil turning stones into bread. Mary was striding ahead, I straggling behind, when we both picked up a powerful odour on the air.

'Cabbage and gravy,' she said, crinkling her nose like a rabbit. 'Floating food!'

We followed the smell into a nearby church hall.

'This is your British Restaurant, duck,' said the woman sorting out rolls of coloured tickets. 'A shilling for adults, half a bob for children. But you're too late for today. Twelve thirty to one fifteen.'

So next day, we went back, each clutching a sixpenny piece begged from Veritas and stood in line to be served a huge two-course meal, cold Spam and two hot veg, followed by steamed spotted dick and custard. It was served out by a band of sturdy women wearing aprons over their trench coats and cotton turbans over their hair. You sat at folding card-tables with green baize tops. You had to eat fast. As soon as the canteen dinners were done, it was time for Baby Welfare when they gave out the orange juice and cod liver oil. After that it was Whist Club.

We went every day that Veritas had sixpences to spare.

Soon, a second miracle event happened. A food parcel

arrived, a tough cardboard box stencilled on the side, *EGGS, with care.*

'What's it say?' Mary demanded.

'Eggs,' I read.

'Eggs? Can't be. You must've got it wrong. People never post eggs. They'd smash.'

The other words on the box were in joined-up writing. This was harder to read. But I knew it was addressed to us.

Mary opened it. 'Because I'm the eldest.'

Inside were six sections lined with corrugated cardboard. Safely cocooned in each space sat a brown freckled egg just begging to be boiled for three minutes like Granny did them so that the white was set like vanilla milk jelly, and the golden yolk was runny.

Mary and I gazed at our gift casket. One egg still had a fluffy white under-feather stuck to it.

'Three each,' said Mary.

I shook my head. 'No, she'll want us to share.'

So Mary and I stopped thinking about three delicious eggs each, and thought instead about one-and-a-half delicious eggs each. That'd still be a feast. But when Veritas saw the box she said,

'Goodness no. Fresh eggs are far too good to be plain boiled.' She said they must be baked into a cake, to share with our new neighbours. 'Like casting our bread upon the waters. And the butcher, we better take him a piece too. Because he's always so friendly.' The butcher sold bags of bones to his regular customers, at tuppence a pound to make into soup. He wasn't to know that Veritas hadn't a clue about soup.

All too soon, we'd be having to share more than a few eggs with more than one gaunt silent father and one fluffy excitable mother.

'Isn't this exciting? Like Christmas Before The War!' said Veritas as she lined up her collection of food colourings in their little glass phials. Red, blue, purple, green. She pulled over two packing cases so that Mary and I could watch the cooking magic. 'You'll both need to give it a wish and a stir.'

Somehow I knew that no amount of wishes would make the alchemy work. Mary whispered, 'D'you think she's ever baked a real cake before?'

The moment the sponge was out of the oven, Veritas painted the top with purple food colouring straight from the bottle, then sprinkled crushed saccharine sweetening tablets over it. Mary said the purple stuff looked just like the stuff that Granny put on our cuts and grazes when there wasn't any iodine.

'Like potassium permanganate?' said Veritas. 'Of course it doesn't. It looks like lovely coloured icing.' Icing sugar was another of those Before The War items that got talked about but made little sense for surely icing would be cold, not sweet?

'I followed the recipe exactly,' Veritas proudly told our father. He was offered the first slice.

'My dearest sweetheart, it's like ambrosia from Mount

Olympus,' he said, smiling at her with devotion.

But he didn't eat it. Mary and I finished it off later. The six-egg cake tasted no worse than the eggless dripping cake which Meg once made at Christmas.

There'd been no message with the eggs. But we knew they were from that distant land flowing with milk and honey, dripping with butter, where ripe fruit dropped off the trees into your hands. And as for the hens, they must have gone back to laying tidily in their coops again.

A week later, Granny posted us a bag of sweet chestnuts. Alas, the hessian had a hole in it so only the bag and half a dozen nuts actually arrived. Then two game-birds turned up, unwrapped, still in their glowing coloured feathers, bound together by a noose with a brown label flapping round their necks like evacuee children had to wear.

'Pheasants!' said Veritas with delight. 'Falcon must've shot them. That means he's back safe and sound!' She sent Mary down the street to knock on all the doors till she found a neighbour who could lend an onion and a rasher of streaky to baste the bird.

Next, it was a fluffy dead rabbit, its hind-legs twined together, its nose dripping blood on to the lino. We watched as Veritas tied on her pinny, and stripped the bunny of its fur.

'Crumbs! That was quick!' said Mary, for once impressed by our mother's kitchen skills.

The rabbit lay across her lap, naked, sinewy and pink-skinned ready for the hot-pot.

'It looks just like a little dead baby now, doesn't it?' Mary said whereupon, Veritas fainted on the floor.

'The rabbit was all right. But there must be something wrong with her,' Mary reassured me.

There was. And a few days later, we were bundled without any clear explanation on to a train to go to our grandparents. Veritas bought us a comic for the journey.

'Just a short stay,' she called through the carriage window. 'So you can get a breath of fresh air. Remember to get off at Spellingly, won't you? You don't want to be carried all the way to Eastbourne.'

Mary buried her nose in the middle page of the Beano, refusing to say goodbye.

'And Mary, perhaps you could try really hard with your reading while you're away? Just for me?'

The train hissed and started to jolt forward. Veritas waddled along the platform alongside the train trying to keep up. What was wrong with her? She was walking like daft Amy. We soon left her behind.

I read aloud the Beano words which looped out of the comic characters' mouths. They mostly spoke in capitals. Mary could do the pictures by herself.

I'd learned to read years ago, quite without trying. One day I definitely couldn't. The next day I could.

'But *how*?' Mary wondered.

Reading wasn't something you could explain, like unpicking some knitting so as to be able to show how you'd got there in the first place.

'It happened in church,' I said trying to be helpful. 'It was something to do with the singing.'

No time to explain more for I saw the SPELLINGLY railway sign sliding slowly past the window.

'Quick! We're there!'

'I know,' Mary said, annoyed that I'd noticed before her.

We scrambled for the compartment door.

'Aaha! here you are, my precious darlings!' Granny was on the platform to welcome us, still wearing up her Women's Royal Voluntary Service uniform, because she was remembering that *Waste Not, Want Not* was a virtue. One embrace from her, grazing our faces on the harsh tweed, some ankle-nips from Jonq and Pol and we knew everything was all right.

'So which d'you suppose it's going to be? The blue ribbons or the pink?' Granny asked.

What was she on about?

'I've bought three yards of each from Mrs Honeysett's to be on the safe side.'

She'd sewn the ribbons into flouncy rosettes, two of each colour, not mixed. They were waiting on her dressing table beside her silver *Rejoice Evermore, Pray Without Ceasing* pin-box. They were to be safety-pinned to our jerseys, in the appropriate colour, as soon as we got the call and heard that the baby had arrived.

'What baby?' Mary and I said together, yet suddenly realising with a sinking certainty why we'd been sent away. We were not to be trusted in the same house as Veritas when something interesting was going to happen.

'Usually a mother must get very fat before she has a baby,' said Mary, trying to unravel for me the mysterious facts of reproductive life. 'Funny how we never noticed.'

The telegram arrived. The message said, 'TRIUMPHANT BIRTH', which meant it was a boy. We were expected to wear blue rosettes all day. Mary unpinned hers and tossed it into the nettles behind the dog-runs.

'That's the limit! I'm jolly well not going to learn to read now!' she said.

'You're probably right,' I said. 'You're not really the type.'

Why do something you didn't like? In church and out of it, she'd always preferred the things you looked at, the coloured angels painted on plaster walls, the stained glass windows, the cherubs in everlasting flight above the white marble knight and his ladye, the carved wooden fruits on the pew-ends, whereas for me, the shapes of words in the books were the main attraction, and Grandfather's sermons which never lasted more than seven minutes because seven was a magic number.

It had been during Mattins that the extraordinary revelation of reading first touched me.

Grandfather had announced the Canticle. The organ had started its deep wheeze, followed by the musical surge. The choir had begun singing the Benedicite with the congregation gradually joining in as they found their places and their voices.

'O all ye Works of the Lord, bless ye the Lord!' bellowed round me.

As usual, I was holding a prayer book up to my face, and opening and shutting my mouth to demonstrate to Cousin Cormorant that, though I might be a drippy girl, at least I knew how to behave in church and not get our grandfather in any more trouble with the bishop.

'O ye Waters that be above the Firmament, bless ye the Lord!' sang the voices. My busy eyes, all by themselves, found the black words printed on the tissue-thin paper and knew that they were saying the same thing. It felt like a painless thunder bolt from the Firmament striking me on the head.

'O Ye showers and Dew, bless ye the Lord. Praise him, and magnify him for ever!' said the little shapes. Then the people echoed it in song.

I raced on, line by line, way ahead of the choir.

O ye Dews and Frosts. O ye frost and cold.

I was panting with excitement.

Oh ye Ice and Snow, ye Nights and Days, all were to bless the Lord. Then all ye Green Things upon the Earth, and ye Whales, and all that move in the water.

By the time we got down to telling Ye Holy and Humble Men of Heart what to do, I was so limp with exhaustion that Aunt Thrift next to me whispered,

'Are you feeling all right, Ruth? D'you want me to take you outside for a breath of fresh air?'

O ye lights and clouds! O ye breaths of fresh air!

'No. I'm all right thank you, Aunt Thrift.'

So much glorious blessing and praising! O ye words and phrases, bless ye the Lord! And since then, I was more than happy to share this blessing of reading with Mary.

I was undiscriminating. Knitting patterns, gravestones, Ministry of Food leaflets for new ways with salt fish, were all waiting to be decoded. Mary, unable to decipher for herself, was much fussier.

'That's boring,' she said, when I read aloud, for her entertainment, Granny's seed catalogue. 'Do this. It looks better.'

It was a handbook published by Spillers Dog Biscuit Company about rearing pedigree dogs.

So we settled on the rug before the fire in Granny's drawing room to our discovery of mange, distemper, ticks, and intestinal canine worms.

Such literary contentment wouldn't last. At tea-time (hot buttered toast, full-cream milk, warm from the cow) Granny had news which we received with poor spirit.

'So there you are, girls! Your mother's managed to get a call through and she'd like you back on Tuesday. You'll both be dying to see the new baby.'

This was her nineteenth grandchild. It put her ahead of Mrs Honeysett who ran the village store. At least someone was pleased.

That Sunday, I was only half listening when the Collect was read out, but I heard enough for its words to jolt me into consciousness of my failings. It was a reminder about casting away the work of darkness and putting on the armour of light.

My own armour was definitely riddled with rust holes for I knew that if the triumphant boy was even a small bit like my Cousin Cormorant, it was going to be impossibly hard to love him as a brother.

SIX

Such Bonny Babies

We were returned like bits of baggage, accompanied by a half a dozen *EGGS with care*, some Victoria plums in a Kilner jar which leaked on to the floor of the train, and daft Amy as our chaperone, for Granny was more alert than Veritas to the possible dangers of bad men on trains.

'I'd *like* to meet a bad man,' said Mary. 'Specially if he was a wolf. Be more interesting than a bad baby.'

Already, the baby had infiltrated himself too thoroughly into the life of Veritas, and yelled too lustily if thwarted for us to put him in the dustbin.

'Oh well, we'll just have to put up with him,' I said trying to make my armour bright and to rejoice evermore.

He took up a lot of Veritas's time. But in a brief moment when she wasn't busy fussing over him, I tried to find out how she'd made him. She went all misty-eyed.

'Well you see, Ruth, love is such a beautiful thing, such a wonderful thing, that through its power you can achieve almost anything. Just think of the Creation. I'm sure

Grandfather's told you about the Creation, hasn't he?'

I knew that God was love, that God's love was so powerful that He'd managed the Creation in only seven days which was even more of a feat than writing the commandments on a piece of stone. But that still didn't satisfactorily explain this baby.

Mary ignored him as much as she could. I ignored him when she was watching, and played with him when she wasn't. He turned out to be quite sweet with a dimpled smile and he didn't smell nearly as bad as Jonq or Pol, even when you went close.

'Ruth, you may look at him, but please don't keep breathing over him like that or you'll give him your nasty germs,' Veritas said.

I didn't even know I had germs.

They called him Alfred George, after some famous kings of England. Both parents were as keen on kings and queens, palaces and princes, as our grandparents were on dogs and God. They arranged, through a friend of a friend who'd worked on secret war things with our father, for Alfred George to be baptised in one of the royal chapels.

'Queen's Chapel. Just down the road from Buckingham Palace, right next to St. James' Palace. Designed for the Infanta of Spain,' Veritas explained. 'Isn't that *wonderful*?'

English or Scottish royalty was best. But Spanish ones obviously had their allure.

'But why can't Grandfather do it in Sussex?' I asked. 'He says he does all his descendents.'

'Only when he's not too busy,' said Veritas vaguely.

'But that's his *job*, baptising, marrying and praying. That's what he's supposed to be busy with.'

'Well, it might be awfully tricky for him to come up here, and quite difficult for all of us to get all the way down there. And definitely far too much for Granny to organise.'

She'd never worried about that sort of thing before.

I had a fog of a memory drifting about in my mind of some wall of misunderstanding, some rift between my grandparents and the person their daughter had married. Slowly as the mysterious movements of the Holy Spirit, I realised I had never seen my father visit the rectory, and rarely heard his name mentioned.

For the christening party, Veritas baked another of the nourishing six-egg cakes. Icing sugar was still unavailable, even on coupons. She decorated the top of the cake with a layer of blue-tinted margarine, moulded a miniature baby's cradle from flour and water paste, baked it hard in the oven, hand-painted it with food colourings and set it sailing on the sea-blue margarine. She let us watch, but not help or breathe.

'This is *very* special and I don't want you spoiling it for him,' she said.

She and our father chose for the triumphant boy six godparents, two with distant aristocratic connections. They brought presents (though nothing interesting or edible like sugar or chocolate eggs). They all said how wonderful he was.

'Anyone would think he was little Lord Jesus,' Mary growled.

I agreed it was unfair that he should receive so much attention and we should have none.

'And how come he gets so many godparents compared to us?' I wondered.

One of my godparents was also my Aunt Thrift which had always seemed a waste of an aunt, and one of Mary's was already dead, killed when his submarine was torpedoed in the Atlantic Sea.

'Because he's a boy, and boys *always* get more than girls,' Mary said. 'You ought to know that by now.'

One of the ten commandments, about not envying other people's possessions, came briefly to mind but that was about not coveting your neighbour's wife, ox, or ass, not about your brother's antique ivory teething ring.

However generously you tried to look at it, the christening seemed a lot of fuss for someone so small he couldn't appreciate any of it. He cried all afternoon. He cried all that night too. And all next day. And then Mary cried. And then Alfred George started gasping as well as crying. Then Mary gasped. Then I did. Then we all had something which Veritas called the whooping cough which lasted for weeks.

After the whooping cough, we went on to have something which the nurse at the Welfare Clinic in the church hall called measles. Then bronchitis. Then tonsilitis and septic ear. Then more bronchitis which made breathing painful. And I knew deep in my heart that these diseases, like the plagues of frogs and locusts that God sent to the Egyptians, were a punishment for disobeying my mother by wilfully breathing on the vivid blue cake.

However, like the manna from heaven which God also sent, Granny continued to rain fresh eggs upon us, also rabbits, the occasional boiling fowl, bottled plums, and heather honey to soothe our inflamed throats.

I'd learned, all of a sudden as with the reading, to do a lot of new things. To do up my own shoes (not just the T-bar button-up but the leather lace-ups which Granny had bought), to tell the time, with Roman numerals, to skip with a rope, to French skip, to hop on one leg, to put myself to bed, to get up, to knit, to French knit, to darn a hole in the elbow of a sleeve, to light the gas cooker without setting the box of matches alight.

'Is there *nothing* you can't do?' Veritas said irribily, when I showed her the knitted egg-cosies I'd made out of unravelled socks. I thought she'd be pleased with the way I made things out of other things. After all, it was what she did. Everybody was supposed to *Make Do and Mend* while there were nothing to buy in the shops.

The more *I* managed to do, the more she was perplexed by my elder sister's inability to read. Our father decided Mary must be taken to a specialist. Alfred George and I had to go along too. I wasn't considered responsible enough to be left minding him. Perhaps Veritas knew of the earlier dustbin plot.

The specialist asked Mary questions. I listened. To most of them, she flatly refused to answer or else she gave a deliberately misleading answer which I knew that she knew was untrue. There was only one question which she answered truthfully. The expert, with an exasperated sigh, said,

'Well young lady, since you clearly aren't interested in being in school and learning anything, what *would* you like to be doing?'

She replied she'd rather be sitting in a tree talking to a chicken with unclipped wings. Veritas and the expert exchanged glances.

Then Veritas giggled and said, 'Mary's always been very fond of animals, you know. She gets it from her grandfather. He breeds canaries and rare dogs.'

The expert listened, looked perturbed and wrote something down.

I knew that Mary's answer was a good one. Hens were her favourite creature. In fact, it sometimes seemed to me that she was a lot more fond of hens than she was of humans. It was just a shame there were no live hens for her to be with in the grimy grey of London.

The visit to the expert cost Veritas far more than she was expecting it to, and made little difference to Mary's progress.

Veritas struggled along, valiantly juggling ration books, stoically queuing for bread, mince, sometimes even for potatoes, optimistically attempting to look after her beloved in a house with an unmended hole in the roof. But she wasn't good at it. She preferred making slinky cocktail dresses out of parachute silk and glamorous evening wraps out of curtain cretonne and going out and having fun with our father and his war-time pals.

'There's no need to complain. We're a lot luckier than many,' she said when the rain came in and buckets and potties had to be set on the stairs to catch it. 'Some people still haven't got any homes at all.'

I had an idea. I said, 'Wouldn't it be a good thing if you had a Meg person, or a Harold, like Granny's got, to help you?'

She wasn't pleased. 'How can we possibly afford domestic help when we can scarcely even afford the rent?' she snapped. 'I think you have far too many clever ideas for someone of your age. You'll give yourself brain-fever if you do so much thinking, then you'll be sick and I'll have to nurse you and I'm in no situation for any more of that.'

She never said that about Alfred George when he learned to do new things, like gurgling and blowing bubbles and shoving mashed carrot and rusks into his own mouth instead of having to be fed.

I wondered, if she hadn't ever had him, would she have liked me more and thought the things I did with bits of unravelled wool were good?

'Only if you were a boy,' Mary said. 'I expect the next one'll be a boy too.'

'Next what?'

'Person. She's going to have another baby. Can't you tell?'

She *did* look quite a funny shape. But I thought it was because her latest dress-making assault, using zig-zag patterned upholstery fabric to make a New Look swagger-coat, had gone wrong.

I thought, so that's why she's been so grumpy. I'll have to make allowances, try to be more helpful, but without letting it show because that's what annoys her most.

I said to Mary, 'But we've *got* a baby. What's wrong with Alfred George?'

'I expect she thinks he's so gorgeous,' said Mary through clenched teeth, 'that she needs another just like him.'

Or was it because she thought our father was so lovely that she wanted another just like *him*?

'At least we were here first,' said Mary.

She was. Not me.

So was Veritas going to go on and on like her sister, Aunt Charité, and have to have five boys, one after another?

No. The new baby was a nice little girl who hardly dribbled at all. They called her Blanche which, Veritas told us, in French meant 'white' which seemed an odd choice of name since she was mostly pink and red. Red curls even when she was only one month old, red eyelashes, red eyebrows, scarlet cheeks and a bright pink bottom.

Now at last Veritas would explain to me properly how babies were made.

'I've told you before, Ruth. You can't have a baby without love. Love is the most important thing there is.'

Despite her nappy rash, Blanche had a wonderfully bonny nature. This was just as well for the whooping cough and other plagues was only the beginning of the seven lean years, just like they'd had to put up with in Egypt in the times of Moses.

SEVEN

In Sickness and in Health

We were a weedy lot, in and out of hospital like yo-yos. The slightest sniffle swept through the household and turned into someone's raging infection, though these illnesses usually missed out afflicting the students who now lodged in the basement, and on the top floor where the rain came in.

'Exactly like the Egyptian plagues,' I said. 'God's frogs rained not upon the chosen.'

Mary was less convinced that there was any connection with the Old Testament. 'It's more likely,' she said, for even if she couldn't read she had a scientific approach, 'that the lodgers are stronger than us because they've been building themselves up on blackmarket food. You should see the tins of stuff they've got hidden under their beds.'

Alfred George was first of the family to be rushed off in an ambulance, though without its silver bell ringing which seemed a shame. When he was allowed home, he looked a bit grey and his pretty curls had lost their lustre. Veritas made even more fuss of him than usual.

Then it was baby Blanche, gurgling as merrily as ever, who was wheeled at a run in her pram to Emergency.

Apparently, it was the high fever that made her seem so cheery. But since she was too young to know how to speak, you couldn't easily tell she was babbling delirious nonsense. That's what Veritas said anyhow when she was reprimanded by a nurse for not bringing the child in sooner.

Then Veritas herself went bright yellow all over, even her eye-balls, as though she'd gilded herself with one of her food dyes.

'Just a touch of flu,' she said, trying to sound brave. But it must have been more than that for she was put in quarantine which meant no one was meant to go near her, apart from our father. He took her cups of tea with a handkerchief over his mouth.

There was a brief lull when the only disturbance was Mary spraining her ankle. She had to be taken to Emergency to be X-rayed, then bound in pink sticking plaster.

Finally, it was my turn.

I'd been taken to Out-Patients to undergo a strange prodecure with heat lamps, as bright as sunlight, directed on my skin because I was taking so long to recover from the plagues sent by God.

'It's to build up the Vitamin D,' the nurse told Veritas. 'Otherwise she'll likely end up with rickets.'

But while I was in the Sun-Ray Clinic with my clothes

still off, a different doctor saw me and changed the diagnosis. He listened to my chest with a stethoscope and decided it wasn't just a lack of Vitamin D that could be cured with a bright lamp.

With a quick stroke from a black fountain pen, I was changed from Out-Patient to In-Patient and was made to stay behind while Veritas went home.

The Sun-Ray nurse kept calling me, 'Rebecca, pet, there there.' So I was sure they'd got the wrong person as well as the wrong plague. But they hustled me away anyhow and shut me into a cot with clanking metal sides which were hooked tight from the outside so I couldn't let myself out, not even to go to the lavatory.

When I complained and shook the bars, a stern nurse wearing a huge white head-dress, came rustling over. 'You're not *meant* to get out! If you want wee-wees, you'll have to ask for the bed-pan.'

The bed-pan was a flat tin chamber pot. You had to sit on it in your bed. I said that it was disgusting to have a potty in the bed. 'Nearly as bad as *peeing* in bed.'

But after several hours, I couldn't hang on any longer. I had to do as they wanted and sit on their tin pot with the boy in the bed opposite watching.

In the morning the first thing I saw through the bars was a woman in an overall, at work with a metal bucket and a long-handled broom. She took a handful of something damp, brown and sticky from the bucket. It looked like the round balls of mess which the milk-horse left down the centre of our road. The woman scattered the stuff around the floor, shoved it this way and that with her broom, then carefully swept it up again. The crisp nurses in their spotless aprons starched as stiff as cardboard, stepped over, taking no notice. The bucket-woman smeared the entire floor of the Princess Elizabeth Sick Children's Ward even into the sluice room and nobody stopped her.

She worked her way nearer to my cot. It was bad enough being caged. I didn't want horse droppings under me as well.

I said, 'Not today, thank you,' in the firm voice Granny used to the gypsy women selling clothes pegs.

She did it anyway. 'It cleans up and lays the dust, duckie,' she said. 'You won't never get well if you're in a dirty old ward, will you now?'

The mess was used tea leaves. She collected them from all the wards except ours (for poorly children weren't allowed tea).

Nobody explained what was wrong with me, when I might get better, any more than they explained that used tea leaves were a substitute cleaner for a hospital which was so poor it even had to save money on disinfectant.

The boy in the bed opposite who liked watching my confusion eventually said, 'You're only in for Obs.'

'What's that?'

'Observation. They look at you and write it down.'

'How d'you know?'

'It says so on the end of your cot.'

After a few days, the Ward Sister said, in a syrupy voice as though offering me a knickerbocker glory, 'We're letting you go home today.'

Veritas, no longer yellow, appeared with my clothes in a paper carrier bag. She said, 'It'll be too far for you to walk.'

But it wasn't quite far enough to be worth the expense of a taxi.

'So I've brought the baby's pram for you.'

How could she have thought I'd agree to climb in and be pushed? It'd be worse than being put in a cot. I refused to get in. But it was a long trudge home for both of us. I was breathless and leaning like a drunk on the pram handle. So was she.

The next day, I thought I must be better, even though it was dark and damp and Novemberish.

'I know!' said Mary. 'Let's cheer ourselves up by pretending it's summer and we've got a big garden.'

So we went out to play tennis in the road with two warped rackets Mary had dug up off a bomb-site. 'Looting' it was called during war-time and she could've been shot for it. But not any more.

'We'll take off our shoes,' Mary said. 'If we wear just socks, it'll feel more like having plimsoles.'

There was no traffic. The only danger was breaking somebody's window. But with a water-logged sponge for a ball, even that seemed unlikely.

Mary tied a length of string across the road.

'That's the net,' she explained. 'If a car comes along we

untie it.' But the only vehicle wanting to cross our court was the milkman with his horse and cart. After a while, one of the young men from our basement came out. I thought he was going to criticise our special method of umpiring. But he simply asked if he could feel my head and take my pulse.

One of the other lodgers had been watching us. It was her idea. His hand felt nice and cool. I was feeling hot and shivery. It was because of wearing socks on a damp road.

'I must advise you to take your sister indoors,' the young man said to Mary. 'It's my opinion, she should never have been sent home in the first place. It was much too soon. They were asking for trouble.' He made me seem like one of Grandfather's prize terriers being wrongly released from its enclosure.

'Don't listen to him. He's not a real doctor,' Mary reassured me. 'He's only a medical student.'

We'd seen the human skeleton he kept in a box under his bed. He said it was a female and he called it 'Mrs Rose'.

It was mid-afternoon when the not-real doctor had felt my head, late afternoon when one of the other lodgers yelled at me to come in, to get into bed and stay there till a proper doctor came. I was beginning to feel a bit weak so I didn't complain, except to point out that I was hungry and I hadn't had any tea. No one made tea that day. Or supper. It was rather odd, specially when I realised that the rest of the family, apart from Mary, had disappeared.

Mary was annoyed with me for going in. 'A person can't

play tennis on their own,' she grumbled. If only she'd learned to read, she'd have had something to do. As it was, she leaned against the bed thumping the racket on the eiderdown.

It was practically dark when I heard our father come wheezing up the stairs. He sat on the edge of the bed to get his breath and looked quizzicaly at me through the glass monocle he wore in one eye. Then he patted my hand in a friendly way. He'd had flu as well as having to put up with his beloved wife being yellow with jaundice so I didn't like to tell him about not having had any tea.

'Not long to go now,' he said, which didn't make any sense.

It was late when a real doctor came to look at me. He said to my father, 'I suppose it'll be easier all round if they take her back in.'

I told the doctor about being hungry. He laughed and went away.

It felt like after midnight when two ambulancemen arrived. I heard them clomping up the stairs with their stretcher.

'Why, it's only a wee girl we've to collect!' one of them smiled. 'I thought it was a woman in labour.' And he took the stretcher down again. The other wrapped me in a red blanket and carried me in his arms. I would have much preferred the stretcher because Mary was standing at the front door to wave me off. Riding in a man's arms was even more lacking in dignity than being put in a cot.

My father travelled in the ambulance with me. This was odd. Normally, he kept well away from us when we needed looking after and specially when we were ill. On arriving at the Emergency entrance, more adults asked my father questions which were difficult for me to understand and for him to answer since they were concerned with personal bodily things and allergies and previous illnesses. Finally, my father was asked, 'Has she had her bowels open today?'

He raised the eyebrow above the eye which wasn't wearing the monocle and looked at me. I had no idea what my bowels were and how they could be opened. But I could tell that my father knew and preferred not to say.

'No,' I answered for myself, hoping that would be the end of the matter. 'Definitely not.'

My father said, 'These are not the type of things a father discusses with his daughter.' Then he kissed me sedately but tenderly on the forehead and left.

I told anybody who passed by the trolley on which I lay that I was still hungry.

'You moaning minnie! You'll get your supper as soon as you're up on the ward,' I was told.

No such luck. When finally I was wheeled back into the dismal Princess Elizabeth Sick Children's Ward, the lamps were already dimmed and the other white mounds were lying doggo. After lights out, nobody dared whimper or thrash about. I longed to be back in the crowded bedroom with my own two sisters, hearing the familiar night snuffles they made. Even Alfred George's rattling cough would have been a comfort.

I whispered to the nurse who was putting me into a hospital gown, 'I'm ever so hungry. I haven't had any tea, or anything.'

It was the same nurse who was so stern the first time I arrived. 'Well, you should've thought of that before you left home. It's much too late now. Supper was hours ago. The kitchens are locked. Look, all the others have gone nigh-nighs in noddyland. So you be a good girl too.'

I stopped yearning for home life. I was too angry. I'd been cheated of my civic rights, persuaded by a young man who wasn't a real doctor to stop playing tennis, forced to go to bed by a mere student, made to think about my bowels in front of my father, and totally abandonned by Veritas. Where was she? How could she have let this happen to me? Mothers were supposed to protect their young.

I became self-pitying. The stern nurse slid through the shadows with her torch and told me to be quiet.

'I am being quiet.'

'I expect your mum'll be in to see you tomorrow,' the nurse whispered.

I doubted it. If she'd allowed me to be left here a second time, she was hardly likely to come and take me away. Perhaps she didn't even know where I was. Perhaps my father had dropped into The Drayman's Arms on the way home. Then, even if she came home, he wouldn't be there to tell her where to find me.

Perhaps I'd have to stay here forever.

I decided that, even if she did come next day, I must refuse to speak to her.

In fact, she came long before morning. The clock on the wall said it was ten past two. She was waddling silently, bare-foot, towards me across the dustless tea-clean lino.

'Sssh, don't let Sister see I'm here,' she said.

What on earth was she doing, without any slippers and in her silk nightgown billowing out and catching the air just as though it was still a parachute floating earthwards?

'Nearly there,' she said. 'I thought a walk would help things along. Better go now, before they find me. Sleep tight.'

She kissed the top of my head and disappeared into the corridor.

She didn't call again. Visiting hours were rigid.

'It's bad for sick children to see too much of their families,' said the Ward Sister. 'It hinders recovery.'

'No it doesn't,' I said. 'It stops them feeling lonely.'

There was half an hour's visiting each afternoon except Thursdays when there was no visiting at all, rather like early closing days when you couldn't get into the shops. If your family couldn't make it during the permitted half-hours, that was tough luck on you. It was the way the nurses preferred it.

'Visitors only make our children cry.'

I didn't wish to be one of 'her' children. I vowed that however bad things were, I wouldn't let her see me cry.

Somebody knew I was imprisoned. A brown corrugated *EGGS with care* box arrived. I saw it sitting under the lamp on the Ward Sister's desk. I heard one of the nurses reading my name off the address but I never saw the eggs, not even to look at.

The next thing Granny sent was a blue paper sugar bag filled with soft green moss. Cocooned within the moss lay a posy of Christmas roses, the white petals as delicate as snow. The nurse showed them to me, then took them away to dispose of.

'No flowers on the ward, dear,' she explained. 'They give off bad fumes, and that'd give us all a nasty headache.'

The Christmas roses in the glass vase in Granny's drawing room never gave any one a headache. Nor did the tall spiky gladioli in summer. Nor the Lent lilies at Eastertime. If flowers gave people headaches, then the whole of Grandfather's congregation would be in agony every Sunday.

The worst part of the illness was yet to come. Soon after the flowers were thrown away, the injections began. Someone discovered penicillin. Someone else developed it into an effective drug that cured everything. It was administered by injection. The fluid was thick as custard. The needles had to be fat. They felt like the tines of a fork trying to pierce my bottom, specially when the nurse was inexperienced.

Four times a day, I heard the crackling apron draw near with the tin kidney-dish in which the cruel syringe lay. As the apron reached the bed, I became paralysed with fear, breathless with panic. But I would never cry.

Out came the instrument of punishment and was held up to the light with the same reverent movement that Grandfather, before the altar, lifted the communion host from the silver paten and held it out for all to see. 'Feed on Him in your hearts by faith with thanksgiving.'

I flattened myself beneath the sheet. I tried to think of Jesus and of His great mercy protecting me. But the mercy was not there. I strained to summon up the four radiant angels who were supposed to be round my bed night and day.

The nurse's hand stealthily drew back my protecting sheet, leaving me exposed and vulnerable. Any angels who might have been guarding me from harm, dissolved into vapour. I'd failed to achieve an acceptable enough level of righteousness for them to stay.

I knew, without a doubt, that the continuing illness was punishment for wrong-doing, if only I could remember what the trespass was.

EIGHT

Like Lost Sheep

There were no books, no toys. We must lie still until we recovered. Days slithered by, lonely and long with nothing to do except think.

Or pray.

Praying passed the time. At least I knew how. Long ago I'd been taught. It was best done in the evening before you went to sleep, just in case you died in the night. Granny said you should kneel by the bed. Veritas said it could just as well be done lying down under the eiderdown.

'Place your hands together. Close your eyes. And if you can't remember any words, speak to God inside your head in your own words.'

Easy-peasy.

But there was a hitch. I had nothing to say. There were no prayerful words left inside my head. Even the Lord's Prayer had long since gone.

Just one line remained, stuck to the inner walls of my skull like porridge on the pan.

'We have erred and strayed from thy ways like lost sheep and there is no health in us.'

At first, I could hear Granny's low voice joining in. But it faded and there was only my own tiny squeak, repeating again and again, 'And there is no health in us.'

In the war, there were no clues, no pictures, no books, to remind me of other prayers.

Had I been sent to where there was no God?

All other periods of my life had been marked by a recognition, however faint, of the existence of the Almighty. The clock in the High Street, which struck the hours, was fixed to the tower of the church, from which also came the sombre tolling for services. At school, we prayed *en masse* twice a day, whether or not we believed, and on Fridays we sang praises to the Lord.

At home an engraving of St Augustine's church hung in the hallway to remind us of Grandfather's parish. The Salvation Army marched down the street, to hold sing-songs on the corner outside The Drayman's Arms. And on wet days when the soldiers of Christ couldn't come, then an itinerant preacher set up his orange box.

At the rectory there were, naturally, even more reminders. Palm-frond crosses left over from Easter on the dresser, wooden crosses dangling from nails on walls, a mansized cross-shape which Grandfather had crayoned on his study wall, hymn books gathering in piles in the hall, awaiting collection and distribution. And every day punctuated by Grandfather's departure, limping gently down the drive, his ankle-length coat over his long cassock, to take Mattins or Evensong in one of the chapels which served the outlying hamlets of his parish.

Here in the ward were no such clues that anybody had ever heard of the immortal everlasting being previously known to me as God.

One afternoon, the frosted window nearest my bed was left half an inch open. For the first time, I could see out. I caught a fleeting glimpse through the narrow gap of a figure scurrying through the rain in long black skirts, carrying a book and a box.

'Look!' I hissed to the boy in the next bed who so liked staring at me. 'A vicar, coming in to see us!'

Hurrah. A bit of praying and singing at last.

In Sussex, the sick got their breath of God with the holy sacraments taken right into their homes. On the kitchen table, Grandfather cut up part of the breakfast loaf into tiny cubes. Half of the cubes went into his pocket for his mice, the other half into his special box with a cross on top to be blessed and become holy. But this was not Sussex.

Before the boy next to me had time to turn his head to take a peek through the gap, a nurse rushed over and slammed the window down.

'Now then, Miss Ruth Nosey-Parker. That's quite enough of that. You mind your own business.'

'I thought he was coming to see us.'

'Of course he's not. The chaplain doesn't need to come here for you boys and girls. Don't you go frightening the other children like that, you bad missy.'

Few of the nurses treated us like humans. Patients didn't have feelings that could be bruised or ears that could hear. Later, while being wheeled to the bathroom like a deaf dumb animal, I had to listen to two nurses discussing a person in another ward.

'Up on maternity. Didn't you hear about it?'

'No.'

'Massive great haemorrhage.'

I didn't know what haemorrhage was. But I knew maternity meant having babies. They lowered me like a dead dog into a pit into the tub.

'So what happened?'

'She had the chaplain brought to her. Last rites or whatever they call it. Her husband insisted.'

I realised you had to be practically dead *and* a grownup, before you could expect a visit from a vicar.

'That's the trouble with this new welfare business. Some of these families, they're just *making* themselves ill so they can come in for free. For the novelty, I suppose. Personally, I don't hold with this National Health. Soon we won't be able to keep them away.'

My parents were socialists. I'd heard them say it. I'd heard them talk of a welfare state. So had they brought our family's plagues upon us by their political views?

'We have erred and strayed like lost sheep and there is no health in us,' was still rattling through my brain.

As I was lifted from the water, now more like a half-drowned cat, I dared to ask the nurse with the slightly softer face, 'Do they ever have hymn-singing here?'

'Singing?'

'Like Sunday school or something?'

'Not now, dear. It's not time.'

'She's an impatient little madam, is that one.'

'Christmas, that's when you'll get your singing. Carols round the tree. It's lovely, with all the consultants in funny hats.'

They took me back to bed. They tucked in the sheets so tightly I could hardly breathe or twitch my toes. That's the way they liked us, flat and immobilised like fallen scarecrows.

'What was she on about?'

'Oh she's just a little worrier, that one.'

'Miss Hoity Toity, I call her.'

The nurses moved on to the boy in the opposite bed. At least when my sheets were tucked in tight, he couldn't try to look up my gown. He disliked being escorted by two burly nurses to the bathroom even more than I had.

'Come along now, Robbie!' they bullied. 'Don't go thinking you're someone special. You haven't got anything down your pyjamas we haven't seen before!'

Now it was my chance to stare and grin at him. It made a change.

'You've a visitor,' a nurse told me when the weekly bathing ordeal was over.

I looked with hope across the ward towards the closed

swing doors where a jostle of waiting relatives were peering through the round windows. Regular visitors didn't waste a moment of the precious half-hour. As soon as the klaxon sounded the start of visiting-time, they burst in through the doors and surged across the lino. But there was no one for me.

'No duckie, she's outside the window,' said the nurse. 'You better hop out of bed. Then you can give her a wave.' The nurse slid the forbidden frosted window up a couple of inches. If I put my head on one side, I could see out.

There stood Mary, in lieu of a parent, on the cinder path. She was staring up at the building trying to work out which window I was behind. I stuck my hand out through the gap and flapped.

'They won't let me in! The beasts!' she called. 'I've brought you a Dandy!' She waved the comic at me. 'They said you have to be over fifteen to get in.'

There were high railings and a deep basement gulley separating us. I had to shout for her to hear me.

'You should've borrowed Mum's lipstick!'

'What?'

'Make-up!'

'I hate that kind of thing!' she shouted back.

'Or high heels then?' She was wearing my old pixie hat that I was used to wear when my infected ears were bad. Her brown woollen stockings were slipping and wrinkled round her knees. She had no gloves. I could see her chilblained fingers, red and blue. If only I'd knitted mittens out of unravelled wool instead of spurned egg cosies. She looked like one of those stateless waifs escaping across a European border with a handcart. I felt sad for her. At least it was warm in here.

'What for?'

'To make you look more grownup.'

'Why should I look like what I'm not?'

'If you'd looked older, they'd have let you in.'

Perhaps she didn't want to be let in. 'Mum says she's sorry she hasn't been to see you. She said she popped down your first night. She thought you were probably too ill to notice.'

'No. I saw her.'

'She's been very busy with the new baby. Then she went yellow again. So did the baby. They wouldn't let her do anything. She's all right now. The new baby's better too.'

Why did she keep saying 'new' baby? Blanche was hardly new. She was nearly one.

'What new baby?'

'It's another girl. They haven't decided what to call it. She had it the night you went off in the ambulance. I thought you knew. That's why we were playing tennis.'

How could Veritas have had another baby without me noticing? I must learn to be more observant.

Mary called, 'You *must've* noticed. Everybody *else* did. It's been very embarrassing. The neighbours keep offering us things.'

'What sort of things?'

She shrugged. 'I dunno. Blankets. Old clothes.'

She'd brought me a conker as well as the Dandy. But we couldn't think of any way she could get them over the railing and in through the tiny gap under the window-frame without them dropping into the basement below.

'If only we had some rope and a pulley,' she called, 'then we could fix something up.' She put them back in her pocket to take away again. 'I'll save them for you. Better get going before it's dark. They might wonder where I am.'

Was it her own idea to come and find me? That made me feel good, at least for the time being.

GRANNY'S GIRL

NINE

To Lie Down in Green Pastures

It felt as though I'd been in hospital for several years rather than three months. So I could hardly belive it when Nurse Grim told me. 'You're going to be discharged today.' She was trundling round with the breakfast trolley. 'So let's hope this time you manage to stay away!'

It was a quarter to six, not even beginning to get light outside when they woke us for cool grey porridge which was even gluier than Veritas's, cold beige bread with margarine. No tea. No soft-boiled egg.

So I lived through another day of waiting till someone turned up with some clothes to fetch me home. It was the lodger who was a medical student. He offered me a piggyback.

I said, 'No thanks. I'm not lame.'

Tied to the front door knocker with a shoe-lace, there was a brightly coloured-in message. I knew by the spelling and the detailed decorations that Mary had done it.

'*Home sweet home. WELCOM RUTH*'. There were

sunflowers, silver leaves, curling tendrils, unidentifiable rainbow birds, crimson rats, dogs, ants, beetles and hens woven round the misshapen letters.

Inside, the house was crowded. There were more student lodgers than before. There didn't seem to be anywhere for me to sit, let alone sleep. After giving me a hurried hug, Veritas said she'd make me up a special kind of bed. It was to be in the downstairs room where she kept her typewriter, the pram, the sewing machine, and where the lodgers put their bikes if they didn't want to leave them outside against the railings. My new bed was the flat-topped trunk in which Veritas stored books, carbon paper, and unperformed drama scripts. She turned it into a bed by spreading a kapok bedding roll over it.

'Isn't this fun!' she said. 'Like camping.'

She put a folding screen round the trunk-bed. She tried to persuade me it was as good as a proper bedroom, perhaps even better.

'See, Ruth, your own dear little corner, just made for you,' she coaxed.

It had been such a long day. It felt as though I'd been on an everlasting journey, between one world and the next. Wearily, I crawled under the eiderdown. At first, it was like sleeping in a passage. There was much coming and going, and clashing of pedals. Later, after everybody had finally gone up, it was dark and lonely. I tossed and coughed on my own. I almost wanted to be back in the other world of the Princess Elizabeth. At least there I had my own bed.

'Couldn't I be upstairs with the others?' I asked next day.

'You know there isn't enough room for all of you,' said Veritas.

That wasn't the real reason. She didn't want me in the same bedroom as Alfred George or the two babies in case they caught my germs. They weren't letting me back at school yet either.

Roundabout elevenses time, it started raining. Veritas had to bring in the nappies off the line even though they weren't yet even half-dry.

'You're going to find it very dull here,' she sighed. 'I don't know what you're going to do with yourself all day.'

Everything used to be such a lark. What's happened for her to be grumbling so?

'Too many people,' Mary said. 'That's the trouble. She can't cope.'

Did she mean too many children, or too many lodgers?

It was a squeeze fitting everybody round the kitchen table. Our father didn't eat with the rest of us. He had his meals on his own, off a plate balanced on his bony knee.

Mary said, 'I expect she'll have to start getting rid of some of us soon. To make it less crowded.'

'She couldn't,' I said.

'She might have to. Remember what happened to Hansel and Gretel? And the woodcutter's son, taken off into the forests to fend for himself?'

I shouldn't ever have read stories to her. When you read to yourself, you know it's just words printed along the line.

But if you *hear* a story, you think you can see it happening for real.

So who would Veritas choose as the sacrificial lamb?

It couldn't be either Mary or me because we'd been in the family longest. Nor Alfred George because he was the only son. So perhaps it would be one of the lodgers, or baby Blanche or the smaller baby, who was still so new she hadn't even got a proper name yet and was called the baby baby. Veritas and our father had been so convinced that with three daughters, they must be going to get another son that they'd only thought up a list of kings' names. None of them was suitable for a daughter.

But how could they send away either of those two defenceless little babies, so young and so pretty? And how could it possibly be any of the lodgers who paid their two guineas a week and fed their silver shillings into the gas meters? And it couldn't be Mary who was usefully strong (apart from her sprained ankle) and could change pooey nappies and fill feeding bottles for baby Blanche.

I knew it would have to be me. I wasn't surprised when it was.

In a flat unfun voice, Veritas explained, 'It'll be fun for you. Like going on an adventure, all by yourself.'

Mary tried to jolly me along. 'You could always pretend you're in a fairy story like the woodcutter's son, and you've got to drop pebbles out of the train window so you can find the way back. You're quite lucky. I wish it was me going to stay at the rectory.

'The rectory?' I said, surprised. If that's where I was being banished to, it wasn't so bad.

'You should be pleased.'

'I am, now I know. But it'd be better if you were coming too. I'll be lonely on my own.'

Veritas said she was taking me as far as Victoria Station on the bus. She was pretending to be immensely cheerful.

She said we should travel on the top deck. 'It's always more fun on top! You can see so much further.'

I wasn't up to appreciating fun. It was more than my legs could do to plod me to the bus stop.

'You're a big girl now,' Veritas told me at the station when she'd found an empty *Ladies Only* compartment. 'So you'll be quite all right, so long as you sit tight, don't talk to anyone and remember when to get off. You'll find Granny'll be there to meet you.'

She gave me a beef dripping sandwich in greaseproof paper for the journey, the old copy of Dandy which Mary had already tried to give me once before, and a rapid hug. I wanted more than that. I wanted her to stay, to sit down beside me, to come too so I'd have her all to myself, no sharing her with a brother and three sisters.

She couldn't wait till the train left. 'I'll find the guard and tell him to keep an eye on you.'

I knew she had to get back to feed the baby baby. It had to be done every few hours, otherwise the baby baby wailed. Lucky baby baby. At least it was getting enough attention. Mary told me that if Veritas didn't feed it regularly she cried too, because the bosoms got too full.

'Full up to bursting unless the baby sucks,' Mary had said, half giggling, half shy, and crossing her arms over her own front. Somewhere under her clothing, she was wearing a sturdy white cotton brassi're. Even through her clothes I could tell.

'Your shape's different,' I'd said accusingly.

She didn't want anyone to notice.

I said, 'Where d'you get it?' I meant the girly undergarment, not the new shape.

'Granny. She sent the money. She said it was high time. And suspenders. She'll probably get the same for you while you're there.'

No way. I wasn't ready for this awful growing-up process.

Veritas walked away down the platform backwards, waving all the way till she was past the ticket barrier. I watched her strange flowing coat made out of zig-zag cushion-cover material moving into the crowd. No one else in the whole station was wearing such a coat. She was a brilliant midsummer blossom being swallowed up by dull grey leaves.

The train didn't move. The compartment stayed empty. I was at no risk of disobeying Veritas by speaking to strangers. No guard came to keep an eye on me or check my ticket.

I watched the train on the next track pulling slowly out in billows of steam. Eventually, a grand woman wearing a feather hat like a brown hen, and skin-tight leather gloves, slid open the door of my *Ladies Only* compartment. The train finally got moving.

Don't speak to anyone, Veritas had commanded. I took good care not even to look at the other traveller in case I felt tempted to speak. I edged my paper carrier nearer to the compartment door so I'd be able to get out quickly.

Just before Spellingly station, the train passed a cowbyre in a field. I stood up. I was ready. The train didn't even begin to slow down. We whooshed past the platform and continued chuffing relentlessly on towards the forests of outer darkness. I knew she'd put me on the wrong train. But why? On purpose? To test my initiative? Or just for fun?

I peered out through the streaky window.

Madam Hen-hat glanced over her fashion magazine. I would not disobey Veritas.

'Excuse me, my dear. Were you hoping to alight at the last station?'

I glared, lips firmly closed.

'Was that where you wanted to get off? Is that where you live?'

I shook my head. Of course I didn't live at a railway halt. I didn't actually any more know where I did live. Probably nowhere. I was an outcast.

'Is-your-family-from-there?' She spoke clearly, separating each word. Perhaps she thought I was dumb or daft. No harm in that. Amy was daft. God still loved her.

I shook my head, then nodded. I really wasn't sure if I even had a family, not one which wanted me.

The woman said, 'I do believe you're from the St

Augustine's rectory. I'm sure I've seen you in church. Don't worry. I'll soon sort you out.' She stopped talking as though I was deaf, more as though making calculations in her head. 'The next station's mine. My man will be there to pick me up. I'll see you home. I only hope your poor people aren't too frightfully anxious. I believe I worked with your grandmother in the WRVS, you know. Such hideous uniforms we had to wear, nearly as bad as the land-girls.'

The train rattled onwards into the unknown dusk. When at last we pulled into a halt I'd never heard of, the lady's shiny Armstrong-Siddeley was waiting right outside. I knew that's what it was because she told me. I said nothing.

She put me to sit in front beside the chauffeur. 'So you can show Jenkins the way.' She settled in the back behind a glass screen.

Her chauffeur was a canary-fancier. He knew his way along the narrow lanes to St. Augustine's rectory even in the dark. He'd once swapped a breeding hen with my grandfather. We swished up the drive, round the oval lawn, to the front door. Jenkins hopped out and pulled on the bell-handle.

After a long wait, Granny opened the door. She was wearing her blue indoor hat and her single-string pearls. But that didn't meant she was going anywhere. She always wore them. She looked with surprise at the chauffeur.

'If you need the rector, I'm afraid he's out with the Boy's Brigade,' she began to say, then saw me. 'Why, it's tomorrow darling, that's when you're arriving!'

She bent down to embrace me. I felt the softness of her cheek. I heard the clack of her pure white china teeth. 'But it's lovely to see you.' Jonq and Pol came bounding down the hall. They dribbled and yapped their excitement.

Granny invited the lady in, and the chauffeur too, which annoyed the lady.

'Jenkins could perfectly well wait in the car,' she muttered.

Granny offered them both tea. The lady declined. So Jenkins had to as well.

Granny said, 'The wrong train *and* the wrong day! Whatever next?'

'The poor child was most terribly brave,' said the lady.

'Dear naughty Veritas! Always in some kind of a pickle, isn't she?' said Granny as though speaking of a not very naughty child. 'Never mind. You're all right now and your bed's made up. Though I better pop the pan in to warm it through.' She meant the long-handled metal warming-pan filled with hot embers which she believed was somehow less dangerous than a stone bottle filled with hot water.

As for my being put on the wrong train, she seemed to find it most amusing. After a while, perhaps I would too.

'But the little poppet!' said my saviour under her chicken hat and the leather gloves which she peeled off like an outer skin. 'She could have ended up almost *anywhere*! If she'd fallen into the wrong hands, *anything* might have happened to her! Heavens, it doesn't bear thinking about, not when there's all that terrible white slave traffic business going on, does it?'

Granny smiled, somehow neither agreeing or disagreeing with the delicious prognostication of terror. Curiously, I felt I could read Granny's mind. She was thinking, Yea, though Ruth shall walk through the valley of the shadow of death, she will fear no evil: for thou art with her; thy rod and thy staff they comfort her. But where had the words sprung from? And why hadn't they been there in my head when I'd needed them in hospital?

Granny was grateful but not effusive. The lady had done what should be expected of any mortal. In taking care of each other, people were carrying out the Lord's work. As a result, I'd come to no harm, neither with abductors at Eastbourne, nor with germs in the bad times in the Princess Elizabeth.

Since they wouldn't take tea, Granny took Jenkins into Grandfather's study to admire the latest canaries, and the lady into the conservatory to select cuttings from the *plumbago auriculata*. I snuggled up among the friendly, dog-smelly, dog-hairy, cushions on Granny's sofa. I was safe, I thought, for the Lord was my shepherd. All the words I needed began coming back. I shall not want. He maketh me to lie down in green pastures. He restoreth my soul.

I heard Granny show the Lord's servants out of the front door. Oh yea, it is good to be here. Where everything is familiar, where the drinking water in the tumbler is cloudy and sandy, and the foaming milk fetched from the farm has little flecks of straw dust floating in it, and where the fire crackles and spits embers on to the rug, and where Granny, absolutely unchanged, is my rock of ages.

'I'm putting you in the Blue Room, since there's no one else here at the moment,' she said. 'I've taken the Valor stove up.'

Such an honour. The Blue Room was reserved for visiting bishops, with the double bed so high you had to take a run at it to climb on, the long mirror in which a bishop might admire his fine black gaiters and purple silk dicky, the patterned Persian rug, faded, threadbare, but grander than plain wooden boards.

But alas, even with the Lord as my shepherd, being in the Blue Room didn't last long into the night. The tall wardrobe began to leer down at me. The wind howled down the chimney cackling like a goblin. The hard bolster beat my head and began suffocating me. Someone started screaming between my ears.

TEN

The Favourite

The screaming was me.

It woke Granny. It woke the Pekineses downstairs in the back scullery. It woke Grandfather. It eventually woke me, though not before Grandfather had limped along the landing in his short nightshirt to carol out into the darkness, 'May the peace, peace, peace of our Lord be with all, all, all who dwell in this house!'

And not before Granny in her long Wincyette nightie with her fluffy white hair down round her shoulders, and no teeth so her cheeks seemed as soft as velvet pancakes, had come shuffling along the top corridor with her candle and coaxed me out from the delirium.

Grandfather went to calm the Pekes with sugar lumps even though they were not his own dogs, but his wife's. Granny dragged the old camp-bed out of her dressing-room and into her room. She placed it alongside her high mahogany bed so that the blankets were touching.

'Then if you need me, I'm right here beside you, darling,'

she said. 'Just give my blanket a tug and I'll wake up. And even if you don't get worse, I can still keep an eye on you.'

How could she do that? Her wire spectacles were on the wash-stand beside the teeth in the tumbler. Without spectacles, she saw no more than the blueness of light and shade.

But *I* could see *her*, and could see the coal-tar lamp to ease my breathing glimmering in its saucer in the grate. I could keep an eye on the great Wincyette bulk of Granny above me. Later in the night, the doctor was called but I was unaware of his visit.

When finally I woke to daylight, she'd long since set off for the cold kitchens, for the finicky lighting of the paraffin cooker, the feeding of hens and dogs, the preparation of Grandfather's kedgeree ready for his return from the eight o'clock. I'd missed the ritual of her dressing, her cold-water *toilette*, and her prayers. But she'd left her wireless on low. The shipping forecast provided a reassuring litany.

'High north west, finny stair by oh six,' chanted the solemn voice from within the Bakelite casing. 'Ninety-nine, developing ninety-nine four hundred. Forties forth! Crometty time! Dogger, fisher, German bite.'

The strange, mystical psalm conveyed the terrible power of the Holy Ghost moving over the waters of the deep.

Grandfather had once warned me that you had particularly to watch out for that German bite, also for Dogger who was closely related to The Dog in the Manger, who refused to share anything with anyone else and so missed the chance of sharing his manger with the Christchild.

Granny's bedroom was peaceful. Beyond the intoning from the wireless, the only sounds were the cawing of the rooks and the faraway barking of Grandfather's terriers in their runs.

The house was so quiet it seemed as if every room, cupboard, cubby hole and closet was dozing. I knew that Meg, the scullery maid, and Harold, the out-of-doors manservant, were still around. But the evacuees, the homeless, the German POWs who'd been incarcerated for so long behind the barbed wire, the assorted hanger-on, had long since flapped off to new perches. Yet, on my own in Granny's bedroom, berthed alongside her empty bed, the only living soul on the upper floor of the whole house, I was less lonely than ever I'd been in the over-crowded Princess Elizabeth.

I watched the cracks in the ceiling and the gentle movement of old cobwebs in the corners of the cornices. Then came a creak of floorboards in the corridor outside and a gust of cool air shivering the webs. The bedroom door opened an inch. A raw grinning face peered round. It was Meg. She'd become more than just the scullery maid who scoured pots and pans with sand. She was now the everything-that-needs-to-be-seen-to-indoors maid.

'Your Gran says to see if you're still in the land of the living. She's popped off down to Mother's Union. And the reverend's at parish council.' Meg plumped up the pillows.

'Ooerh, but Miss Ruth! Whatever've they been doing to you up London? Colour of putty, you are, and that's the truth. Harold could be mending broken windows with you!'

Meg had a tray set with Granny's best, the china plate, the egg-cup, the little cream jug, all patterned with dainty wild violets. A large brown egg, a horn egg-spoon, and a line-up of buttered toast soldiers. Too much. I couldn't eat it though it was lovely to look at. And the white aconites and sprig of pink myrtle in a tiny glass vase.

'That's your Gran, out first thing picking them specially,' said Meg.

Yea, my cup runneth over.

'Nice mug of Benger's to build you up, that's what you need,' said Meg who was obviously going to include being cook, housekeeper and nurse among her domestic duties. 'I'll tell your Gran. And plenty of proper TLC.'

I didn't know what either Benger's or TLC were. But I could definitely feel love lapping round me like little waves on the side of the pond.

There was to be more penicillin too. Mr Dodds, the chemist, notified by the doctor, brought it up from the village himself. But this time, it wasn't in a syringe, just thick and vile in a medicine glass.

'Hold your nose and swallow it down,' Granny coaxed. 'For if you can't smell it, you won't taste it.'

I turned away my face in disgust.

'Now, Ruth, please don't be disagreeable about this,' Granny said more firmly. 'You know there's plenty of little girls in Africa who'd give anything to have a sip of your medicine.'

Granny could be so strict with runaway dogs and disobedient children, yet could also be gentle and patient as though she had all day to fritter away.

'There's my good girl,' she said approvingly when I spluttered down my dose. From then on, she provided the reward of a barley sugar twist for every dose taken without a fuss. I saved the barley sugars under my pillow to give to Jonq and Poly. If I could be bribed, so could they.

'Now I shall read to you,' Granny said when the two o'clock medicine had been dealt with. (Like the baby baby's feeds, the medicine came every four hours.) 'This is called *The Cloister and the Hearth*. A big favourite of mine. I do hope you'll enjoy it too. It's set in the Middle Ages, in Holland, such a romantic adventure, and tells us something of the times and thoughts of Desiderius Erasmus.' I was too sleepy to ask about Erasmus. 'You may not follow all of it. Never mind. Just close your eyes and listen anyway.'

The book, from her own childhood, was bound in faded red, with dulled gold lettering on the front and back which caught the light from the fire. The print was small. She had to push her spectacles up on to her forehead and hold the page right up to her nose to see it.

'Botheration!' she muttered. 'I knew I should've learned my favourites off by heart when I still could, like Mother told me.'

I fell asleep in mid-read. It didn't matter. There were

more chapters the next day. Even though she had so much to do in the household, the garden and the parish, she made time for reading. I couldn't remember Veritas ever reading aloud to me.

The Water Babies followed. 'I know you've read it before, darling. But a good story can always stand up to a second hearing, can't it? D'you remember how poor little Tom had to climb the dark dirty flues to brush them clean?'

I did.

'Such a splendid Christian clergyman that was!' she added. She meant the man who'd written the story, not Tom the chimney sweep.

Then came the *Children of the New Forest*. 'About the English Civil War. Oh, it's so exciting, darling, specially when they have to hide up in the oak to escape the Roundheads!'

To be read aloud to was as wonderful as good dreaming. No wonder Mary liked it. I'd had no idea. Up to now I'd always had to be the reader, never the listener.

Occasionally, Grandfather came and read some of his serious sacred verses or, even better, nonsense rhymes about invented animals which Noah had left out of the Ark so they drowned in the flood.

Gradually, through lying back and doing nothing, I began to re-find the person I was before. Ruth had not, after all, dissolved into the blank invalid inhabiting Bed Sixteen in the Princess Elizabeth but was still here waiting like an embryo. The inner Ruth was still lacking in grace, still occasionally thirsting after righteousness, the better to be loved by Granny, but definitely still there.

'You know what, Granny?' I offered one afternoon when the small print seemed particularly troublesome to her and she'd had to cross to the window to hold the page up to the light. 'I could read aloud to you instead?'

'Not yet. You have to rest. But maybe tomorrow, or the day after, if your temperature stays down, you shall come to the drawing-room for an hour or two. I'll build up a good fire. And the dogs would be pleased.'

So, wrapped in Granny's mohair dressing-gown, I was installed like a princess on the saggy chintz-covered sofa. My retinue had escorted me downstairs. My consort, Granny, supported me by the arm, the courtiers, Harold from outdoors and Meg, my new and kindly nurse, followed with blankets, stone water bottle, and pillows. Granny brought her potted lilies in from the conservatory and placed them on a console table so I might observe the blooms unfold. A china chamber pot was hidden for my use behind the spinet on which Granny used to accompany hymn-singing long ago.

'There we are now, my own Ruth, little and good, that's you,' said Granny, tucking me in.

Oh how I warmed to her approval, how I loved her love.

After the move to the drawing-room, my reading repertoire broadened. I started by reading everything that had slipped down the back of the sofa, or lay on the floor within arm's reach. The Illustrated London News, a prayer book which had been waiting to have its torn pages repaired before it had slipped into oblivion, the new plant catalogue with crosses marking Granny's spring bedding plans.

'Ooh what a little bookworm you are, Miss Ruth!' said Meg with admiration. She didn't read more than necessary. She preferred rag-rug-making.

'But Ma goes for the reading, just like you,' she said. 'There's nothing she loves more than a good wallow.' Meg brought me a stack of yellowing, dog-eared magazines. 'Ma says she's done with them now. Only catching the dust back home.'

In *Women's Friend*, *Women's Weekend*, and *Woman and Girl*, I learned about a chirpy kind of home-making that never happened at the rectory, and probably not in Meg's home either. I saw, as though looking through the wrong end of Granny's binoculars, into a compact world where you could turn a man's head if you fashioned yourself a saucy sailor hat out of a scrap of leftover gingham, where you could brighten a dingy bed-sit with a lick of distemper, where you could create your very own Coronation souvenir out of a cheap tin-tray from Woolies, some glue, and a couple of your favourite royal pinups snipped from the picture weeklies. There were stories too, about love. But I skipped those.

Soon I was strong enough to potter across the drawing-room and select volumes from Granny's shelves. I hauled back to the comfort of the sofa, the hefty thousand-page Army and Navy Stores catalogue with which Granny had done her shopping when first she married. And so I learned the 1909 prices of feeder wicks for oil lamps and mantles for gas lamps, whether purchased by the dozen or the gross. Then I skipped my way through a biblical concordance, tracing with my eye the maps of Palestine under the Herods, and checking the frequency of references to Frankincense in both Old and New Testaments. Next came the nine hundred and forty-nine close-packed pages of *Mrs Beeton's Book of Household Management* where I learned the duties of the footman and how to prepare mock oyster pudding, to plan an October dinner for eighteen, to carve and quarter a haunch of mutton, whatever that might be. Meg didn't know either.

Eagerly I went on accumulating my rag-bag of unrelated facts. Veritas used often to laugh at my ignorance of general knowledge. One day, perhaps there'd be a chance to show her what a lot I now knew.

Aunt Thrift came to stay. She inspected me curled up with Jonq and Pol on her mother's sofa.

'She looks all right to me,' I heard her say with a disapproving sniff.

'Why yes, she is, isn't she?' Granny agreed. 'Improving every day. I'll soon get the roses back into her cheeks.'

'But shouldn't she go to school?'

'Oh no,' said Granny. 'She's learning all the time.'

And so, in a way, I was. Everything I read, cookery tips, geography of the Holy Land, management of domestic servants, stirred around inside my brain like one of Mrs Beeton's extra-rich plum puddings. But though it made me feel full and happy, I began to doubt if it would actually alter Veritas's opinion of me.

'Cocky and too clever by half,' I could already hear her scoff.

Just as I was beginning to feel the first twinges of boredom, Cousin Faith arrived from her boarding school. Her father, Uncle Kestrel, had a new posting to Singapore. He wouldn't be back for three years. So Faith was going to have to spend every holiday and weekend *exeat* here at St Augustine's. She didn't seem too pleased about it. She sauntered into Granny's drawing-room to look at me.

'Gosh, you're so damnably lucky!' she complained, practising a new mature word which she'd never have used if either grandparent were in the room for there was no swearing, drinking, smoking or gambling at the rectory. (Nor were there any card games, apart from Happy Families.)

'It's just not *fair*! It's never been fair with your lot. Specially you. You get to lounge about and be waited on by Meg while the rest of us slog away. I had to help polish all the altar brasses this morning. *And* I had to walk those revolting hounds.'

Lucky Faith. I was longing to race about outside with the dogs. I tried to croak back that it wasn't my choice to get my lungs riddled with infection like rust-holes in tin cans. But I hadn't the breath to get into a discussion.

'You've *always* been spoilt, my mother says so,' Faith went on. 'You're Granny's favourite. I'm sure you must be. She even buys you *shoes*!'

I couldn't deny it. And vests.

I wanted to tell Faith that Granny had even bought my sister suspenders and a brassi're, but then the words stuck in my throat. Commandment Eleven says thou shalt not flaunt to thy first cousin about items bought by Granny.

'What's all this?' said Faith, noticing barley sugar wrappers on the floor. 'Sweeties too?'

'For the dogs,' I whispered, wriggling further under the rugs so there'd be less of me visible to annoy her. But the wriggle brought on a coughing fit. I had to sit up again.

Faith took a sip from the tumbler of barley-water before handing it to me. She must have been expecting something delicious. She made a face at the musty taste.

'Dishwater!' she said, spitting it over the fireguard and into the fire.

For the rest of her stay, she kept away, except at story-reading time. I was relieved to see that Granny bought her some new Chilproofe woollen underwear. Granny's choice in vests was uncomfortably long (to protect the kidneys) and with ugly little cap sleeves.

A week after Faith had left, Cousin Cormorant turned up. He'd changed. He wasn't so crowing and argumentative, just distantly tall. Or was that because I was down on the sofa and he was standing up? He was into men's long trousers. They were too long and wrinkled over his shoes which were enormous, like leather arks.

'Hello old bean. Taking it easy as usual, I see,' he said with an irritating grin. 'How's that scrumptious sister of yours?'

'Don't know. Haven't seen her for weeks and weeks.'

'Ah well. By the way, got an air-rifle now. Perhaps you'd tell her.'

Obviously, I was meant to be impressed, or Mary was.

'Granny says I'm not to bring it indoors, otherwise I'd show you. But she says I can have a pop at the squirrels. They're stealing all the fruit from the loft.'

So I didn't see much of him either, though I heard the busy crack-crack as he aimed at rodents. The sound sent Jonq and Pol crazy with excitement. They yapped at the conservatory windows until Meg came and let them out, then raced off to pretend to be Cormorant's gun-dogs.

I could bear their wretched faithlessness. I could cope with anything, just so long as life went on exactly like this, for ever and ever in my cocoon of perpetual security.

ELEVEN

Friends and Revelations

The thirst for miscellaneous knowledge wasn't easily slaked. I fluttered continuously along the bookshelves, not so much a bookworm as a book butterfly, sipping nectar from here, there and everywhere. On one of my rummages, I came upon three flimsy exercise books tucked away behind Granny's gardening guides. They were marked 1897, 1899 and 1901, in inky black.

I flicked one open at random. The writing was careful with lots of elegant loops and swoops.

I fear I don't lead as good a life as I might (I get so slack), I read.

But I've been settling down to steadiness again although I don't do lessons in the schoolroom so much, now I have a pony. It is to help me get out and take exercise. Since my recovery, for which I give thanks to the Lord, I've begun the year with a great deal of thought – I think that during the last few months my brain must have begun to enlarge or do something. I've got a perfect mania to know more – and to read everything there is. But where to start?

I shut the note book. This was someone else's private thoughts. I felt they could almost have been my own (apart from the pony).

'Can I read these?' I asked Granny. Although she'd said I could read anything, it was safer to check. Veritas used to say I could read *anything*. Then when I read a page of one of her playscripts as it rolled up over the typewriter platten, she told me not to be such a nosy snooper.

'What is it, dear?'

'Someone's personal writing, I think. It looks old-fashioned.'

'I expect they're Uncle Guillemot's stories. Or your mother's. They were always scribbling away as children.'

It didn't look like Veritas's. Her writing was scrawly. She wrote everything in such a hurry. That's why it was easier to read after she'd typed it on to her Remington.

'Let me have a look dear.'

I handed Granny the exercise books. She glanced at a page of the neat script.

'Well, fancy that! Those old penny books! I do believe they were mine! I can't have been much older than you. I wonder how they got there.' She pushed up her spectacles to peer more closely. 'I was terribly ill once. Then they got me a pony. I was always writing about him. Poor old piebald. He didn't last long. On his last legs when he came to me. Yes, that's copperplate writing. We had to do it in the schoolroom with those dreadful dip-and-scratch nibs. Such a trial, specially the pot-hooks.'

'Pot-hooks?'

'Downstrokes. Look. On the g's and y's. Yes of course you may read them. It was my mother's idea I should keep a journal, like the young princess Victoria. Though I don't suppose you'll find them very interesting.'

Not interesting? Anything about her was interesting.

I retreated to the sofa with the penny books. It was clear that my Granny had always been good, even when she was only twelve or thirteen.

Grandmother says to me, 'Trust ye in the Lord for ever' – But it is so hard to trust – It is hard to remember that the Lord is always there & ready to be trusted. I pray for things & hope that by some remote chance they will be granted. But I don't trust.

She wrote about going to prayer meetings, reading her Bible, and doing useful tasks to help the people who lived in the neighbouring cottages.

Today I went to see our old people. Oh I do adore them!! Yet I am so afraid of simply gossiping with them. I heard some one say about a girl the other day, that she simply went to see them to catch the latest gossip but I try to go for something better although I think their talk & little tales are fascinating.

When she felt she wasn't being good enough, she urged herself to try harder.

I have done so few acts of self denial this year. I had 2 factory girls down but they were no bother. It was only the paying for them, so I can hardly call that a good work of self denial. Then I have had the Rectory children but as much for my own pleasure as to help the rector's wife. Then I've done a few tiny self denials, very small (generally duty) and very seldom, barely one a day.

I must put down what things I mean to do better–

I   *To give up more & self deny more*

II   *To be nicer to Mother (I have been horridly cross & sharp & rude to her lately, so dreadful to Mother, though Sarah says this is only because I am sickening for something & that the sick may be bad-tempered)*

III   *To be more careful what I say about other people*

IV   *To get up earlier*

Meg came in with another steaming mug of Benger's food. So I shoved the penny books under the sofa cover. The imagined imperfections of the rector's wife were not something for her to know about. I waited till Meg had put another log on the fire and gone out before retrieving the notebooks.

I read about the loathsome lessons in the schoolroom, the dislike of visiting curates, about educational visits to the local brickworks, and how much she wished she could go away to school like her brothers. Then came the illness and she wrote nothing for weeks and months, until a sudden outpouring.

This morning I suddenly thought, supposing I had died when I was so dreadfully ill with the scarlet fever and then the rheumatic fever when my joints were so painful? Wouldn't it have been funny – I should have been dead all this time, dead now, this minute – the others wouldn't have known me as I am now & I shouldn't have known them. They'd only remember their young sister and they'd have to put flowers on my grave.

But Jesus didn't let me die. Why was that? Had he something special for me to do? I wonder if it will be brave and exciting or steady drudging service?

As I read this, I wondered if her life had indeed been saved for 'something special'? And if so, was it to be here now to save *my* life? And was this a 'brave and exciting' task or only a 'steady drudging service'?

The eggs, the milk, the early-to-bed, the steady loving care continued. The penicillin, too, must have done its work. I knew I was getting better. I could feel energy beginning to tingle in me like spring sap rising in the trees.

Waiting for Meg, I bounced up and down on the sofa instead of lying limp and still.

'Blow me, don't jump up and down so, Miss Ruth! Or you'll be scalding yourself and me into the bargain!' Meg scolded. 'Looks to me as though you'll soon be ready for a breath of that fresh air your grandmother likes, just to calm you down.'

Granny agreed.

She wrapped me up like a party pass-the-parcel in multiple layers of clothing: two vests, a jersey, a windcheater jacket, her old gardening coat, and one of Uncle Merlin's boiled wool balaclava helmets which had seen wartime service. It had tiny holes which could have been made by bullets, but Granny said was the moths. Everything was held in place by a mohair muffler criss-crossed over my chest like a bandolier. Then she let me out to walk Jonq and Pol.

'Once round the walled garden. Then directly back. We don't want you catching a chill on your kidneys on your first day.'

I survived the walk without dying of exposure or heat stroke. She let me trot down to the Home Farm with the can to fetch the milk. The air was crisp. The old chestnut leaves of last autumn were iced with a sherberty rime. I kicked through them with my spindly legs and saw the sturdy green spikes of snowdrops already pushing up. I felt reborn.

Then it was back indoors for another of Meg's nourishing hot drinks. Meg put as much trust in the powers of commercial beverages as Granny did in the Lord.

'Drink it up. Bovril keeps out the cold,' Meg quoted the maker's slogan off the side of the jar, proving she could perfectly well read. She just didn't enjoy doing it as I and her mother did.

By next day, I was in and out through the back-door running errands for Grandfather. I gathered mulberry leaves for his silkworms, and groundsel for his canaries. To Granny, common groundsel was a raggedy weed invading the kitchen garden. To caged birds it was a delicacy. Grandfather rewarded me with sugared almonds which were dusty from being stored beside the hamster meal.

A few more days of errand-running and Granny decided I was strong enough to go down to St Augustine's and help polish the brass eagle on the lectern. But inside the church it was as cold as being underwater and just as hard to breathe. My wheezes echoed round the effigies.

'You had better go outside where the air's warmer while I finish off, dear.'

When she emerged, Granny wandered over to inspect the flowers displayed over a recent grave.

'Such a nice one from the nurses,' she said of a wreath of hot-house white roses. 'So generous. The poor dears can hardly afford it on their wages. But they said they were really going to miss him. I don't know why. He was ninety and quite dotty.'

While I read messages of condolance, Granny tidied round other graves, emptying jam jars of mouldy water, flinging withered flowers on to the compost heap.

'Fancy leaving it like this!' she said, gathering up an armful of rusty green wire frames and yellowing laurel leaves. 'It makes our churchyard look so untidy. What will visitors think? I'd better go and have a word with Hedger.'

She talked to the old man who scythed the grass between the tombstones. I rummaged through the heap behind the yew tree and salvaged some of the frames to see if I could make anything useful from them. Then I visited my favourite grave. Elizabeth Anna was a baby who'd died thirty years before. The granite slab marking the spot was less than two feet long.

'Yes, I remember the night she was born,' said Granny. 'What a struggle she had getting into the world. Less trouble leaving it. She'll be a little angel now, dancing in heaven.'

I wondered how someone who hadn't even learned to

walk while alive, would know how to dance when dead.

Although Granny talked tenderly enough of angelic infants, there was no such sentiment for the elderly.

'Who's it for?' I asked of a new hole being dug by Mr Hedger.

'Only old Bell from Squirrel's Wood. Thursday. And high time too. He's kept everybody waiting.'

She showed me the place she was saving for Grandfather and herself, a quiet spot within the shadow of the church, close by the grave of the long-ago baby girl, such a fine plot that one of the parishioners had tried to take it over.

'Old Mrs What's-her-name from the house past where we get the cowslips. She's not even been in the village that long. We've told her she can be buried at the lower end like all the other newcomers.'

On our way home over Starling's Hill, our eyes keeping watch for early primroses, she said thoughtfully,

'You know Ruth darling, all this talk of the old isn't right. And I believe your Aunt Thrift may be on to something when she says it's not good for you to be on your own all day.'

'I'm not on my own. I've got *you*. And Grandfather in the evening. And Meg talks to me plenty.'

Our gossip was mostly of hair-styles, of girdles versus roll-ons, not that Meg wore either.

'Yes darling. But there's no one of your own age.'

'I don't need anyone. Please don't send me back, will you?'

'We'll see,' she said cryptically, which was no answer. 'At least not till Dr Sprott says so.'

Dr Sprott hadn't seen me since the night I was really ill. Long may he stay away.

That evening, just as the clock in the hall chimed eight, which meant it was time for bed, Granny said into the fire, 'Of course, she should never have married him in the first place.'

'Who?'

'We always knew it was going to be a disaster.'

'But who shouldn't have married who?'

'The others, Thrift, Charité, they did all right. Even Speranza.'

She was talking about Veritas. But what an extraordinary thing to think. How could my mother *not* have married my father? If she hadn't, I wouldn't even exist, wouldn't be standing here now, hesitating in the doorway. How could Granny, who knew so much about the all-encompassing love of our Lord, show so little of it towards her son-in-law?

'Why not?' I said.

'He was too old for her,' she muttered to herself. 'Called himself a writer. That's no proper job for a husband. He had no money. He was quite unsuitable.'

Could she be right? Was he really unsuitable? My loyalties, for grandmother or for father, were being stretched as tight as the rope in a tug o'war. I ought to defend my father against her attack. But how? And what was so wrong about being a writer, apart from the fact that it made a noise? I remembered the friendly sound of his typewriter clattering through the night as he thumped away on the keyboard, creating his plays and poems that never brought in any money.

A long time ago, before any of his children existed, his comedies had often been put on in West End theatres, so Veritas used to tell us proudly. They were about European heiresses, lost inheritances, and royalty attending balls under assumed identities. But it seemed that post-war audiences weren't interested in that sort of drama any more.

'*And* another thing!' Granny added angrily. 'They married in secret! Right in the middle of the Blitz, without telling us till it was too late to stop them.'

I crept up to bed, said the prayers which would keep Dr Sprott away, read three of Meg's mother's magazines, and went to sleep, confused.

At breakfast while stirring porridge on the range, Granny said brightly, 'By the way darling, I've found you a friend to keep you company.'

So at least she wasn't sending me home. But who could it be? One of the cousins? No, they were all away at boarding schools.

'Amy!' I said, disappointed, for being kept company by daft Amy would be like being entertained by an empty wardrobe, large, fusty-smelling, difficult to move about. Then I felt guilty for the disappointment. 'I expect you've asked nice Amy to come up for tea?' I forced myself to sound pleased. 'How lovely!'

'No, it's a new little girl just arrived in the parish,' said Granny. 'Not that her parents are worshippers. Not even chapel. They seem to have a grudge against the Almighty. She's just the same age as you. I met the mother at the Women's Institute. Not that she'll be joining. She came to borrow the big tea urn. They'll be living at the old camp. Just for a while. They don't know anybody and the mother thinks it would be nice for both of you. The girl's been poorly. But I think she's on the mend. Just like you!'

The old Prisoner of War camp on the far side of the village still had men living in it, people who didn't belong anywhere and had been drifting this way and that since the war was over. They'd ended up on the edge of an English village. Granny said they were called 'stateless', and that it was even worse than being homeless.

'Just because they haven't got homes or countries to belong to, they still have to be fed,' said Granny.

The girl's father was in the catering corps. The mother had worked in a wartime canteen. It was to be their job to feed these sad stateless refugees.

So, the new girl was fetched by Meg from the old POW camp and brought up to the rectory, almost as though she was a pony being brought to cheer me up.

I resolved to take as little notice of her as possible. She was going to ruin my peace and quiet. What if she was bossy and abrasive like my cousin Faith? Or wanted to dig up dead moles like Mary?

TWELVE

My Star of Stars

'The name's Vivien, isn't it dear?' said Granny, introducing us with formality. She made us shake hands with one another in the drawing-room. 'And this is my granddaughter, Ruth. I've twenty-three grandchildren. Ruth is the fifteenth. I'm sure you'll have lots in common.'

I didn't think so. She wore three flouncy petticoats as though it was the most normal thing in the world. Her ringlets were tied with white satin bows. She had shiny black patent shoes on her little feet.

She was too shy to speak, and at first, hardly looked at me.

Granny suggested we might like to exercise Pol in the kitchen garden.

'Good idea, Granny,' I agreed, seizing the chance not to have to stay shut up in the drawing-room with this stranger. She seemed the silliest creature I'd ever seen, and so dainty she looked as though she'd break like a china doll. And I did not play with dolls.

As we walked past the dog-runs in the yard, the terriers began their usual frantic barking. They raced like frenzied demons up and down inside their prison fences.

The girl said in a lisping baby-doll voice, 'Why aren't we taking those ones for a walk as well?'

'Because they're Grandfather's. They're show dogs. Mr Harold has to exercise them. They can be vicious biters too.'

We pushed through the wooden door into the walled garden. The girl said, 'What about that other dog we left behind indoors? Doesn't it want to go walkies too?'

Jonquil was on heat. That was why we only took Pol. But did this china dolly girl know about such things as bitches being in season?

I said, 'Pekinese dogs are very fussy. The other one doesn't like going out in cold weather.'

We walked solemnly round the kitchen garden, eyes ahead, keeping strictly to the box-hedge paths because of the girl's footwear. We took it in turns to hold the dog-lead.

'That's a fig tree,' I said. 'At the right time of year, it has figs.'

'That's nice,' she said.

I wondered if she'd ever tasted a fresh ripe fig.

'They're pink and slimy inside. But grownups like them.'

We walked on.

I said, 'And those are the nectarines. Growing against the wall. They like the sun.' And I suddenly wondered why, at the times when Jonquil was on heat, she never tried to mate with Polyanthus who was the nearest male dog in her life. Did dogs have their own morality code about mothers and sons, as Grandfather hinted, or was it that Granny kept a sharp eye on Jonq and Pol and at any sign of sexual affection, separated them? This wasn't something I could ask about. Unlike Veritas, Granny never actually told fibs, but there were some topics of which she said,

'We won't talk about that now, darling. Maybe later.'

How much later? Didn't I need to know everything *now*?

Vivien called again the next day. But it was raining.

Granny said, 'Why don't you two girls play over in the stable loft where you'll be out of the weather?' Then she noticed how unsuitable the visitor's clothes were for climbing a dusty ladder into a loft. She suggested our visitor might like to remove her petticoats and her dancing shoes and put on borrowed galoshes and corduroy trousers.

'And while you're up there, dears,' Granny called after us as we clumped out of the backdoor and through the clucking hens, 'see if the Hunwell Sourings are ready, will you? And if you find the squirrels have nibbled any, better bring them down. We don't want them setting them all off, do we?'

'Yes, Granny,' I said for I knew how one red squirrel's nibble could turn a whole Russet mouldy. And one ruined apple could spread its rot to the entire crop, just like germs and sin.

'I'm named after Vivien Leigh,' the visitor said as we sat

amongst the battalions of green, red and yellowing Sourings, Seedlings, Reinettes and Pippins, lined up on their sheets of old newspaper.

'After what?'

'*You* know, Scarlet O'Hara in *Gone With the Wind*, with that gorgeous big crinoline.'

I knew about dogs and apples but was ignorant of film-going.

Vivien patiently, sweet-naturedly, explained in her soppy whispering little voice.

'See, she's a screen pin-up, ever so famous. She's a real smasher, that's what my dad says.' Vivien was as proud to be named after a star as I was to be named after my grandmother. 'And my daddy says my mum looks ever so like her when she gets her hair up right. Calls her his own starlet. They're as keen as mustard on the flicks. They'd go every night if they could.'

'Why can't they?' In my experience grownups did what they wanted, except for Granny who did what the Lord wanted.

'Got to work, haven't they, you silly-billy,' said Vivien, giving me a hug. 'And look after their cutie-pie, that's me. And anyway, there's no picture-house round here, is there?'

'No,' I said. 'I suppose there isn't.' Not that I'd ever noticed before.

'Dead as the grave,' said Vivien. 'My mum says we saw more life when we were stationed on Shetland.'

At least I'd heard of the Shetland Islands. But beyond

that, I had little in common with this pretty stranger. We weren't even the same age, whatever Granny thought. She was younger than me but so much more sophisticated, what with her ringlets and her petticoats. I stared at her dark wavy hair. So dark. Such lovely rippling waves. And at her fine dark eyebrows creating elegant arches over each pale violet-tinted eye. And at her long dark curling lashes. Everybody in my family had sand-coloured eyelashes, so fair you could hardly see they were there.

'My eyebrows are the spitting image of Margaret Lockwood's, my Daddy says.'

Another star I'd never heard of.

'*The Benighted Stranger*,' said Vivien gently. 'Doesn't matter if you've never seen it, you've probably heard of it.'

I hadn't. 'Er yes, I think so,' I said.

'Margaret Lockwood has an hour-glass figure.'

'Oh. Has she? That's lucky.'

'A beautiful bustline. Have you got a bust yet?'

'I don't think so.'

'*I* have.'

'Have you?' I said.

Suddenly, she leaned towards me and gave me a hug which for someone as small and frail as her, was surprisingly firm.

'Yes. Oh Ruthie, I'm so glad I've found you. I've been ever so lonely for so long. I hate being ill. It's the horriblest thing.'

I thought she was going to cry. She didn't. Instead, she

released me from the hug, smiled at me and said, 'I just know everything's going to be all right from now on because I've got you.'

I felt a mad rush of love for her. I'd never felt like this about anybody before, not even Mary.

With a star's namesake for my friend, my life was suddenly complete.

THIRTEEN

Bustlines

Up in the loft spattered with bat droppings, Vivien unbuttoned her Liberty bodice. Proudly, she showed me the bustline that was going to become a feature as fine as Margaret Lockwood's. Her torso looked little different from my own. Bluish mottled flesh and pinkish nipples, only very slightly puffy.

'I'm afraid I can't see much going on,' I said, sad to have to disappoint her.

She fluttered her lashes. 'But I can *feel* them growing. I pull them every morning to help them along. I hope they come in time.'

In time for what? I said, 'I don't want bosoms. Ever.'

'You shouldn't say "bosoms". It's vulgar. It's "bust" or "chest".'

'Alright. But whatever you call them, they'll still get in the way of dancing and climbing trees and walking dogs and whatever else we might want to do.' I could clearly recall the sight of Veritas hurrying away from me across platform 9 to get back to the baby baby in time. 'The only thing they're any damned use for,' (I used Cousin Faith's grownup word), 'is feeding babies. And even then, it hurts.'

'I don't mind. I'd still like some. They're so grownup. My mum says I've got to grow up fast because there's not much time left.'

'That's what my grandmother says too, that we have so little time on earth. "For man does not know his time".'

'Did you know I'm going to die?'

'We're all going to.'

'Yes I know. But I *really* am.'

Of course I didn't believe her, that Vivien, the new star of my life, was already near the end of hers. It made even less sense than Granny's negative views on my father.

'I've never had a best friend before,' I said, hugging her. I'd had a best sister. I had three friends, Meg, Jonq and Pol. But this best friend business was something new.

With Vivien visiting me every day, life became miraculous. I no longer needed to immerse myself in reading. Instead, we played, as I'd never played before. Even if I didn't understand about Vivien, I understood that my own time was running out for childish games.

Vivien was her parents' only little treasure, not a pretend only-child like I'd become. Vivien loved our make-believe games.

'Keen as mustard, that's me,' she said when we played at 'Coronations', at 'Two Little Princesses and Their Nanny', at 'Surviving the Blitz', at 'Births', at 'Maids and Master', at

'Lost Babes in the Woods', at anything I could think of. One of her favourites was 'Graves', when we died and rose again just as it said in the New Testament we would, only we did it time after time.

'It's scrumptious!' she said. 'I didn't know there were games like this. How d'you learn them?'

'Just made 'em up out of my head,' I shrugged. Had she spent so much time in the stalls with her mum and dad that she'd lost the knack of inventing things? 'Inventing's easy-peasy. Anyone can do it if they try.'

But perhaps not everybody could.

'I never played such smashing games as this, not even in the Peter Pan.'

'In the where?'

'Peter Pan Ward. We went up in the lift.'

'Where was it? In the Shetlands?'

But she didn't know where, any more than I knew the actual location of the hospital I'd stayed in. Ambulances took you there. You were kept lying down so you couldn't see. The windows were darkened so even if you sat up, you couldn't see much.

'What did they do to you?' I wanted to share horrid secrets of needles and tests, fainting and fear.

But that was a game Vivien wouldn't join in. She dismissed her poorly past. 'Can't remember. It was ages ago. Come on, Ruthie. Let's do that other one you told me. "Baptising the baby".'

So we fetched our chubby oak logs from the wood-shed,

wrapped them in sack, and gave birth to them as we lay in the grass so we'd have something worth baptising down by the pond.

Vivien gave her log a baptism of total immersion. 'My Mum and Dad don't hold with this sort of thing,' she said laughing.

She was muddy up to her knees. They probably wouldn't hold with that either.

I knew I was way too old for this kind of nonsense. I shamed myself, even as I gave birth to stillborn triplets.

Roses were growing in my cheeks, just as Granny had predicted they would. But Vivien was always as pale as a wood-anemone and sometimes a little blotchy.

After making three grass-graves for the deceased triplets, she was so exhausted that she had to lie down in one of the shallow hollows to recover. I sprinkled sorrel seeds on her. I muttered some mumbo-jumbo prayers of commital.

'Come on, corpse! Up you get! Time for the Last Day of Judgement. Break free from your earthly tomb. Dance with the clatter of your old dry bones.'

She grinned with happiness but didn't move.

'Are you, O late deceased, a bit of a drip?' I nagged.

Of course she wasn't. Real drips complain. Vivien never complained, even when she was too puffed to move. She sat on a tree-stump and nursed her infant log.

'OK, we'll do the Coronation then and you can be the Queen,' I said. 'Then you can stay sitting where you are. I'll be all the rest of them.'

As the Archbishop, I crowned her with the Royal Imperial Crown studded with its diamonds and rubies and emeralds, and Vivien, in a high queenly voice said, 'Thank you very much, Archbishop.'

We had no idea what might actually be going to happen at the coronation of the real young monarch whose face was on all the tin tea-caddies and tea-trays in Honeysetts' Stores. But in the meadow beyond the pond in the grounds of the rectory, anything could happen that we wanted to. And the only witnesses were the waterfowl nesting at the water's edge.

It wasn't like having a sister. Vivien never contradicted me. We never argued. I began to wonder if it might be possible for us to marry when we grew old enough. My Grandfather said he believed in marriage between all creatures of the same species. So might he be prepared to conduct a marriage between people of the same gender?

Once, Vivien thought up a game herself. 'It's called "Film Stars And Their Best Bits",' she said. 'You know, like Trevor Howard in that bit in *Brief Encounter*. Or *Blue Velvet* and Elizabeth Taylor, or Cary Grant, or Belinda Russell. To make it easy for you, you can choose who you like.'

There was a problem with me playing 'Film Stars'. The only film I'd heard of was *Henry V* because the actress Vivien Leigh was in it and so Vivien had told me about it. I so much wanted to play the game of 'Film Stars' because it would have involved some kissing. I wanted to kiss Vivien. Playing Coronations didn't involve kissing. Queens don't kiss, except on the hand. We both knew that.

'*Gone with the Wind* then?' Vivien had one last try. 'You must know it. Everybody knows it.'

I didn't.

'Never mind. We'll do another 'Graves'. Let's do that old man in the village who sits outside the public house.'

I had another idea, even better. I said, 'Let's do Amy!'

So we both acted being old Amy who in real life was said to be as daft as a brush, although also one of God's special people who needed extra love to make up for the lack of brains. In our game we made her even dafter than a brush, so daft that she tottered along on her wobbly legs and climbed down into her own grave even before she was dead.

Vivien and I giggled hysterically as we lay together in the grass draped in our floral shrouds of chickweed and wood sorrel. But even as we played Amy's Grave, I was ashamed. We were mocking one of God's special people. I knew it was wrong to mock the afflicted, even if Vivien didn't. As a rector's descendent, I should have lead the way in righteousness. Instead, I was heading the way of darkness yet again, letting in sin through the rust-holes of my armour.

And as the public confession stated so clearly every Sunday morning, there was no health in me.

★ ★ ★

I'd known her for only three weeks when she died. It should have made me cry. She'd had something called leukaemia, not one of the words I knew, and she'd had it for a year.

I felt so angry. Why hadn't anybody explained all this to me properly so I could have known not to let myself get too fond of her?

'Peacefully, in her sleep,' I overheard Meg, the all-purpose maid, whisper to Harold as he came to the backdoor for his ten o'clock cup of tea. 'The little love. Her blood's went too white. They knew she was going but they never thought it'd come so quick.'

'And what about *her*?' Harold jerked his head in my direction. 'How d'you think she'll take it?'

Meg caught sight of me skulking in the shadows of the scullery doorway. She fell silent. It was not for a maid but for a grandmother to inform me of the awesome news.

'My first real death,' I told Jonq who wagged her tail and rolled her bulbous wet eyes.

I was impressed by Vivien's audacity more than I was sad. It was such an adult thing for her to have done.

If only Cousin Faith were here, I'd have told her and it would've stunned her into silence, that I'd had a best friend who'd achieved the mystical ultimate.

'I know what a loving presence you were for her, Ruth my dear,' said Granny. 'It will have been such a comfort to her parents, knowing she had you as a companion to the end.'

The hot shame of it. If only Granny knew the truth

of our silly dreadful games in the grazing meadow. I would have to be righteous for the remainder of my life to make amends.

Vivien got to have a real funeral. I was not at it.

Granny said, 'Funerals are no place for a healthy child.'

'I ought to be allowed,' I tried to insist. 'She was my friend. And I was hers.'

That wasn't the true reason. I wanted to see what a funeral was like, what they'd do, I wanted to watch Grandfather standing importantly with his scarlet and black stole billowing in the breeze.

Perhaps the parents didn't want me there? Perhaps they thought if they saw another child looking so well, it would make them upset?

Granny said, 'You're missing nothing. The little girl won't be there. She's already dancing in heaven with the angels.'

'She told me she wasn't baptised. She won't go to heaven.'

'Nonsense. Our Lord doesn't bother about things that like and nor does your Grandfather.'

So Vivien had got to see my favourite infant, Elizabeth Anna, long before me. It wasn't fair.

Granny said, 'Our Lord said the dead should look after the dead. And the living take care of the living.'

I wished I could make myself cry. But thinking of Vivien dancing in heaven in borrowed galoshes amongst the graceful angels only made me want to giggle.

I busied myself making a wreath from yellow colts'-foot and dandelions bound together with trailing strands of vetch, just the way we'd made them for our pretend funerals.

'This is a real wreath for a real funeral,' I told myself. 'I must try to grow up.'

Granny took me to St Augustine's to place it on Vivien's earthy mound. She mistook the silence of my shame for grief.

The florists' wreaths for Vivien were already wilting so that the spiky frames showed through like metal bones.

We stopped at Honeysett's Stores on the way home. Granny said, 'We'll pop in and get some muffins.'

She thought I needed cheering up. We came out with a pot of Yarmouth bloater paste and some chocolate dragées for Grandfather because he too needed little treats from time to time. Once Lent had started, he couldn't have them.

Then we saw daft Amy. She was shuffling about in the twilight by the village pump. She was without her coat or hat.

Granny was sometimes stern, but hardly ever as angry as she now became. 'Really!' she snapped. 'This is too too wicked!'

What was too wicked? That some children were born to die, some were born to get better, and some were born as daft as a yardbroom and never grew up at all?

'Two parents lose the most precious person they have. Others don't deserve what they've got. The way those people treat her!' She was talking about daft Amy and her family.

Granny asked around the village green and discovered that Amy's people had gone to the races for the day.

130

'On the charabanc.'

They'd thought it wasn't a good idea to leave Amy locked indoors in case she got into trouble.

'So they've left her outside till they get back,' said the publican. 'But it doesn't seem quite right, does it, Mrs Rev?'

Granny brought Amy back with us to share our muffins by the fire and to recite Evening Prayers. Amy loved praying, far more than I did.

Later that evening, Grandfather went over to Amy's folks. He made them an offer too good to refuse. Amy was to remain indefinitely (which probably meant forever) at the rectory as an unpaid GH.

'What's a GH?'

'A general helper,' said Granny. 'There's simply loads of things Amy can do, if only she's given half a chance. Can't you, dear?'

One of the things was to keep me company. All evening I had Amy lumbering around beside me like an empty wardrobe.

'How long's she staying?' I asked.

'Well, Grandfather was thinking she could be trained up to feed the hens, and walk the terriers. So at least till we're through Lent. They aren't very nice to her down at her home. She tells me they make her sleep in the shed when it's her time of the month. And she likes it here, don't you Amy?'

Amy made a sort of gurgling noise that was probably a yes.

Next morning, she got to have a three-minute egg with

toast fingers on a Bunnykins plate, just like me.

Granny said, 'Well done, Amy. Now, when you two girls have finished, you can help Meg wash up. There's no reason she should wait on you hand and foot. And then you can walk the dogs.'

Girls? Amy already had grey hairs, on her chin if not her head. She must have been at least as old as Veritas.

But if Granny had decided to love her, then I must too for, as Ruth in the Old Testament says, 'Your people shall be my people.'

But I had much further to go than Ruth, the Moabite woman.

The next day, Dr Sprott was sent for.

From my perch up in the branch of a tree, I saw his small shiny motor trundling up the drive. I saw it chug round the oval lawn to the front of the house. I saw the short, pale man get out. He wore a white wing-collar and black jacket. I knew he was not the bishop. The bishop wore gaiters and a purple silk front.

I stayed up the tree.

But five minutes later, I heard Meg screaming my name from the back door.

'Ruth! Miss Ruth! You're to come in! Your Grandmother wants to see you in the drawing-room! This instant.'

Slowly, reluctantly, I sloped in. As I passed through the scullery, Meg dabbed my face clean with a tea-towel.

'Hello, my dear,' said Dr Sprott, holding out his hand to shake mine. 'And how are you now? Much better than the last time I saw you, I'll be bound.'

When I had undressed in front of the fire, he listened to my chest, back and front, politely avoiding the breasts, first with his stethoscope, then tapping with his cold, very clean hands. He looked down my throat with his torch. He flattened my tongue with a wooden stick. He peered down both my ears. Jonq and Pol watched and twitched their snub noses.

As I re-dressed, as hastily as I could, Dr Sprott chatted to Granny about the dogs and their diet. He didn't mention anything as impolite as bowel movements and kept his eyes well away until all my clothes were back on.

Amy stumbled in with a tea-tray. Meg must have set it for there were the correct number of saucers to cups, and milk in a jug with a net fly-cover over it.

Dr Sprott held his cup and saucer in his clean hands and told Amy how well she was looking. Then he declared that I too was as fit as a fiddle, definitely well enough to travel, to return to school.

Granny smiled. But my heart sank. It was like a death sentence. I'd have to leave.

'Granny no! Do I have to? Let me stay here with you and Amy, just as we are? *Please*?'

But granddaughters did not have outbursts in the drawing-room, specially not in front of a medical gentleman sipping his tea.

'Not now dear,' said Granny calmly. 'We'll talk about it later.'

After Dr Sprott had left, I pleaded and I begged.

'But Granny, you *can't* make me go back there! Please don't. I have to stay here with you forever. She doesn't even love me.'

'Of course she does. In her own way.' Granny drew me to sit on her knee, though those knobbly old thigh bones were too brittle to support me for long. 'I do understand, Ruth my darling, how being the second child can be dismal. I was the second in my family. It's easy to feel over-looked, through no fault of your own, to fail to come up to the parents' expectation.'

Yes, this was just how I felt.

'They're over-awed by the miracle of the firstborn. They forget that their next is just as important. Every child is a precious gift from God.'

'I'm not special to her,' I said, pouting. 'Alfred George is but not me.'

'I believed that my mama thought less of me than she did of my brothers. But that did not mean that I *was* less. So don't be downhearted. The Lord knows your very special qualities, even if you don't yet know them yourself. Now, since this is your last evening, how are we going to make the very most of it?'

I chose. And of course we did exactly those things we'd done for weeks. We sat by the fire while Jonq and Pol snuffled beside us, springing briefly awake when a rogue spark leapt out on to the rug. And we played dominoes. And then Happy Families, then Spillikins. Amy couldn't follow the rules of any game, let alone count the white dots on a domino brick. But she took her turn anyway.

Grandfather joined us after Evensong and listened while Granny read aloud the next chapters of *Down the Bright Stream*.

The companionable evening flowed towards its gentle ending. And I didn't belong here any more. There was no more discussion of the matter. I had to go back to that other life of noise and mess, with grizzling babies and steaming nappies on the fender, with arguments with Veritas, and everything supposed to be fun, shortly followed by neglect and burned porridge. Being the only grandchild was going to be swapped for being part of an overcrowded ark where there weren't enough beds to go round, let alone food.

I wondered how long it would take me to get used to it. And would they get used to having me back?

I did so hope that my mother wouldn't find fault in me all the time. But perhaps it was up to me? I vowed to try hard to meld, to be helpfully invisible, not to complain about the box-bed behind the folding screen, to seek righteousness wherever it was, to rejoice evermore and to pray without ceasing.

But as the train drew into the platform at Victoria Station, my vows floated away like engine smuts into the smoggy air.

YOU'RE A BIG GIRL NOW

FOURTEEN

One of Us

'Whooth thith?' said my little sister, Blanche. She'd learned to talk in whole sentences while I'd been away. And she was no longer called 'the baby'. This was in order to distinguish her from the baby baby, who was now called Felicity which, so Veritas told me, meant 'happiness' in French.

On my first breakfast back at home, Blanche kept pointing her porridge spoon across the kitchen table.

'Whooth thith?' she repeated. And when that didn't get a reply, asked, '*Whath* thath?' as though I were an object, not a person.

'It's Ruthie of course,' Veritas reminded her. 'Your nearly grownup sister.' She'd started to say 'your big sister' but changed it halfway through. I wasn't at all big. I seemed to have stopped growing upwards, though the bust that Vivien and I had searched for had definitely begun. There were two buds stretching the pink skin over my rib-cage. However hard I pressed them with the palm of my hand,

139

they wouldn't stop.

'Thon't need nother thithter,' said Blanche. 'Ith goth thoo thithters. Thaths loths and loths.'

Despite the fact that I brought them the customary gift of six brown eggs and the leaky Kilner jar of plums, the rest of the family treated my return with offhand indifference. It was as though they thought I'd only been away a couple of nights instead of half-a-lifetime, or a whole lifetime if I counted Vivien.

When I muttered under my breath about prodigal daughters returning to the bosom of their family at least getting a proper bed to sleep on, Veritas said, 'Now then, Ruthie, you're one of us. You've got to learn to muck in.'

But a mattress on the floor (I'd grown too long for the box-bed so Alfred George had taken it over) wasn't to be my bed for much longer. Nor was London to remain our family home. No sooner had I learned to 'muck in' (which meant not complaining about beds and doing my turn with the washing-up) than Veritas was announcing the next important move.

'Move?'

'Yes, Ruthie, move!' she said. 'Isn't that exciting?'

'But I've only just got back.' I could hear the whine in my voice. Why couldn't we stay still? Why must she be so restless?

She gave that threatening smile which warned me I was being selfish to consider only myself.

It seemed that it was the unexpected arrival of the new

baby so soon after baby Blanche, and then my recurrent illness, which had made them decide they had to make some major changes.

Mary knew already. 'At least it means I'll get a change of school,' she said gloomily. 'I hate school. They won't let us do Art till after the third year. You have to finish Geography first. They are so unreasonable.'

What had *she* got to moan about? She was lucky. At least she'd been able to keep going to school. I had months and months of catching up to do.

Our father was pounding away at the keyboard of his typewriter balanced on his thin knees. Was Granny right? Was this an unfit occupation for a husband? A glass of beer was balanced on the arm of the chair. It seemed that he didn't go out to the Drayman's Arms any more. The walk made him breathless. Also, it was going to save money and time if he stayed at home and drank beer and wrote his plays simultaneously. What would Granny think of that?

Now, he glanced up at Veritas, twirled his moustache ends and gazed with total approval through his monocle as he did about any of her barmy schemes. But he didn't say anything. He never interfered with domestic management.

He was busy finishing a seventeen-part verse-drama based on a history of Her Majesty's Foot Guards, which magnificently married his interests in things regal and things military. He'd been writing it since long before I was disgraced by sickness and sent away. The drama of the Foot

Guards, Veritas explained to everybody, was expected to make the family's fortune.

'Provided we can find a backer to produce it,' she went on. 'And I'm sure we will. I know we will. The new Elizabethan Age is full of people wanting to invest in the golden future.'

Our father didn't seem to go out to work any more. With the war well and truly won, the government hadn't needed so many people doing secret work.

'So he's gone back to being a full-time writer,' Veritas said. 'Which is the noblest of all professions.'

I knew Granny wouldn't agree. I said, 'Doesn't he need a bit of a job as well?' I wanted Granny to love him as I did, to be as proud of him as Veritas always was.

'Writers don't need jobs,' she said airily. 'We haven't got time. Not with all the writing we've got to do.'

She wrote youth pageants on worthy subjects which were sometimes put on in echoing church halls. Between them, they reviewed other people's books, wrote punchy advertising for a gravy thickening manufacturer, and verse which might one day bring them fortune but never fame, for it was destined to be printed, unsigned, inside greetings cards.

None of the feverish literary activity earned enough money to support seven people. I grew out of my raincoat. I wore through the soles of my walking-shoes. There wasn't any money for replacements, and I began to understand why Granny had been annoyed with her daughter for marrying a writer for love, instead of marrying a solicitor for security.

They'd tried to move once before, to New South Wales. It was on the other side of the world, so Mary warned me. The Australian emigration board was seeking strong farmers and skilled technicians, not writers with dreamy ideas about the romance of history and five hungry children. Our parents' emmigration application was turned down without them even getting an interview.

'So you're home just in the nick of time, Ruthie,' Veritas told me, 'to join in with the fun of packing everything up.'

Is packing fun?

'Of course it is, darling!' For Veritas, even peeling a saucepanful of turnips could be exciting so long as you approached it in a positive and adventurous spirit.

'And the important thing is, this move is going to make us all richer and healthier,' she said.

I didn't see how moving could ever make a person healthy. I tried to explain that it'd been the frequent moving, between home and hospital, between the warm ward and the cold X-ray rooms, between one hospital and another, which had kept making me worse. It was only when I'd been allowed to stay still with Granny that I'd finally got well.

But I had to remember to keep my opinions to myself. When Veritas made plans she didn't like them criticised.

'This is quite different!' she said. 'We're moving to the

country, to Sussex, where the air's really clean and pure. None of us will ever have to breathe dirty smog again.'

'How long for?'

'For ever.'

'You mean we're moving back to Granny's?' I said with a gulp of surprise and delight. Granny must have forgiven our father for failing to earn a proper living.

'No, not to Granny's. I don't think either she or your father would like that. But to a lovely big house quite off the beaten track where you can each have a room of your own.'

'What about all your friends and your cocktail parties? Won't you miss them?'

'Father and I need to get away from all distractions. We want to live a peaceful life, so we can both write more and better.'

For once, Veritas's enthusiastic vision was rooted in reality. The abandoned farmhouse she'd seen advertised was enormous. It was set in an isolated hamlet, and was romantically beautiful in a neglected, ancient sort of way. The farmer it belonged to, Mr Greenfinch, had long ago moved into a new, neat, red-brick bungalow up the lane. He was bemused that anybody should actually want to rent the sprawling old building to live in.

For the first week, Veritas sat at the farmer's wife's borrowed sewing-machine and made curtains out of her cocktail dresses, and lampshades out of her evening wraps, while Alfred George, Blanche, Felicity and I raced about the numerous empty rooms filling them with shrieks and noise.

In the farmhouse there were thirteen bedrooms, a reception room big enough to dance in, a dining hall long enough to seat a banquet for thirty, a parlour, a snug, a pantry, two sculleries, and a quiet panelled writing-room for each parent. But after only one morning of being apart in separate rooms, Veritas and our father found they missed each other too much. So they moved back together to share the same writing-room. Veritas pushed their desks together to sit side-by-side, facing a mullioned window framed in graceful wisteria. Beyond, they had views of trees and fields of contented cows.

'Just right for inspiration,' said Veritas.

There were half a dozen outhouses into which Mary, who considered herself beyond rushing hysterically about the corridors, soon installed hens, a lame goat she bought from a boy passing down the lane, a mongrel bitch in pup which she found in the hedgerow, and two Muscovy ducks the farmer gave her because his wife couldn't bear to eat them. Mary didn't intend to either.

How our parents were going to pay regular rent to Mr Greenfinch wasn't yet revealed. Neither of them had sold a single punchy advertising slogan, or a couplet of birthday-card verse for weeks. Would they be borrowing from Granny again?

'Don't worry your pretty little head about things so much, Ruthie,' said Veritas with a merry carefree laugh.

'I *know* we'll find a way.' She implied that she had trillions of good ideas up her sleeve. 'If Father's new play doesn't make our fortune this year, maybe one of mine will? Or perhaps we'll grow vegetables to sell?'

The magical but overgrown garden of this new home looked as though it needed several months of slash-and-burn techniques before it would grow anything edible, even for the lame goat.

'Or perhaps,' Veritas went on, 'we might open a hotel? Now wouldn't that be fun?'

Did she or our father know anything about hotel management?

'Not an *ordinary* hotel, Ruth.'

I thought, but didn't say, that with her special kind of colour-dye cooking it certainly couldn't be. I put on my how-interesting-mother-dear expression.

'A special hotel for children only.'

I said, I didn't know children ever went to hotels. I certainly hadn't.

'No darling, not *ordinary* everyday children,' she said. She called me 'darling' much more than she used to. Perhaps she, too, was trying hard to ease the friction between us. 'It could be a hotel for the sad, lonely children of the very rich who need a nice holiday in the country. And it'd be such a wonderful opportunity for you and Mary, and the little ones, to share your nice bedrooms with others less fortunate.'

At last I'd got a proper room of my own and already she

was making plans for me to start sharing it. I thought back with a pang of yearning to the quietly lonely evenings spent with Granny, reading by the fire. That time already felt distant, receding into the past. So did Granny herself. We were all now living in the same county, only a dozen miles apart. But Granny didn't come to visit. Perhaps she wasn't invited. Perhaps she was busy in the parish. However, she sent over, by carrier, a crate of Cox's Orange Pippins, a pair of socks she'd knitted for Alfred George, and a hairbrush I'd left behind. Tucked in amongst the aromatic apples was a letter for Veritas. Unfortunately, it was sealed. But from Veritas's expression as she read it, a mixture of annoyance and relief, I suspected it was an offer from Granny to help with the rent of our new home.

And once she'd made enough curtains, Veritas became suddenly more concerned with planning improvements for Mary's and my spiritual welfare than she was with practical details of schooling and rent.

This spiritual improvement would involve a trip over to the rectory, perhaps several.

FIFTEEN

Ratification and Confirmation

'So Father thinks it would be a good idea,' Veritas explained, 'if you and Mary were to go over to Grandfather to be prepared for your Confirmation.'

'*Father* thinks so? You sure?' It seemed unlikely. 'Father doesn't even believe in God!'

Our father glanced up from his typewriter. 'Indeed so,' he said. 'But he does not consider that a valid enough reason for impeding his daughters' pathway to finding true belief. Agnosticism is not known to be hereditary, any more than virtue is.'

Veritas added, less convincingly, 'And I know your father would *like* to believe in God, if only he could bring himself to, wouldn't you, my dearest?'

'Absolutely, my sweetheart,' said our father with scarcely a pause in his typing.

Later, Mary said mournfully, 'It means they reckon we've reached the age of discretion, that we're finally growing up enough to take charge of our own lives. Once you've been confirmed, you're considered too old for your godparents to have to send you presents any more.'

Her godmother was an aristocratic Russian translator who'd worked alongside our father doing those secret war things. She sent Mary an envelope of rare strong black tea-leaves once a year, in time for the Eastern Christmas in January. It made a bitter brew which no one but our father could bear to drink. However, her other godfather, who went down in his submarine, did better in the present line. In memory of the drowning, his father sent Mary a highly useful cheque every Christmas. This was how she managed to buy dog-meal and hen-food, and the furry and feathered livestock she was rapidly acquiring.

My godparents were more prosaic with offerings of girls' adventure books, gift-wrapped soap, compendiums of letter-writing material, and holy cards. But never cheques. So if giving up on presents was considered to be a step towards maturity, I could tolerate it, and even try to do so gracefully. But I wasn't at all sure I was ready to give up the godparents themselves.

'I *need* to go on having them, to know they're there even if I never see them. They sort of bear me up. And I don't feel nearly old enough to ratify and confirm my faith.'

Veritas didn't agree. 'Of course you are. Remember what a lovely little acolyte you were at St Augustine's last Advent.'

'But all those difficult promises. And all those bits about triumphing against the world, the flesh and the devil.' I knew I wasn't ready. There was that terrible dark period in hospital when I'd most needed the grace of God, yet been unable to feel it. I was unworthy.

Veritas threw back her head and laughed like a gurgling brook. She'd done a lot more laughing since we'd moved here. Our father had done a lot more smiling fondly through his monocle. They both seemed much happier overall. And if *they* were happy, then it was good for the rest of us.

'So that's all settled then, isn't it, Ruth?' said Veritas, as though all my doubts and queries about confirmation had been resolved by her merry laughter.

'I suppose so.'

'So just try not to do so much *thinking*.'

'I'll try.'

'Because you do want to be done alongside Mary, don't you? It's good for sisters to be together. I always fought with mine, which was a mistake.'

'Yes.'

'And I know Grandfather would like it. And there may well not be another year for him.'

'Why not?'

'He's well past his three score and ten.'

So was this another reason why the whole family had had to move? So that Veritas could be closer to her father as he neared the end of his life, even if they didn't see eye to eye? And so that Mary and I could be offered as peace-makers before it was too late?

'Not exactly,' said Veritas. 'Though that's important.

After all, he won't last for ever. The bishop says he's got to retire. But you know what Grandfather's like. He says he won't go.'

For our first Confirmation class, Mary and I set out to bike to the rectory. It was a long haul with our bike-lamps flickering faintly into the darkness, but worth it for the lovely tea Granny had ready for us. Eggs, and a fresh comb of honey, and bottled plums with cream.

And then, the anticipation of enlightenment with Grandfather about those mysterious concepts which had been so hard to grasp, specially long ones ending in -ion. Transfiguration, excommunication, solemnization, ordination, circumambulation. All that reading while I'd been convalescent had resulted in knowing lots of words with scant knowledge of their meanings.

After our tea with Granny, Mary and I went and stood nervously on either side of Grandfather's roll-top desk and waited. He had to finish feeding his hamsters, guinea-pigs, silk-worms and canaries first. We listened to the thriving, spinning, chirruping, scrabbling noises of captive life. Even if he didn't get around to telling us the difference between say, transubstantiation and consubstantiation, he would surely explain to us about Creation, eternity and the curiously elusive workings of the grace of God.

'Do you know the Commandments?' he asked at last, shaking flakes of guinea-pig food off the front of his cassock and hobbling slowly back to his desk.

I remembered about not being covetous, nor

blasphemous, and about not murdering your wife, or was it about not selling her?

I nodded. I hoped Grandfather wasn't going to ask me to recite all ten Commandments in the right order. Mary, more wisely, shook her head and said, 'No.'

Grandfather said, 'There are two Commandments. First, though shalt love the Lord thy God with all thy heart. Second, thou shalt love thy neighbour as thyself. See if you can remember those two. And now for some sweetness.'

And that was it. One class only. Our official preparation was over.

Grandfather directed Mary over to the hymn book cupboard to fetch out a bar of chocolate peppermint cream. It looked like the remains of one, and slightly stale. Perhaps a free-ranging hamster, or perhaps Grandfather himself, had nibbled one end. With his rusty pen-knife, using a dusty postcard as a plate, Grandfather sliced it into three.

'And lo, the Trinity!' he said like a conjurer at the end of a trick, handing us each our one-third portion. 'One piece of peppermint cream can also be three.'

As we pedalled home through the dark, I felt less ready than ever for the bishop's visit. Would the bishop be convinced by the peppermint cream explanation of the mystery of the Holy Trinity?

But we were on course. There was no backing out. Granny had already bought us new shoes, sensible brown brogues so they'd do for school afterwards. Mary's had a special firm instep inserted to support her weak ankle.

'We're going to look very peculiar wearing clumping shoes under white dresses,' I said to Mary, for I'd supposed we'd be dressed like miniature brides in white organza with veils and flowers. But it seemed that Grandfather didn't approve of such flamboyance. We were to wear Sunday best – grey stockings and grey pleated skirts which Granny had made up for us by Mrs Honeysett's niece who'd recently re-covered the drawing-room sofa.

The finished skirts turned out to have more the appearance of a pair of comfy tweed armchairs than of young person's apparel. Bunchy valences rather than pleating hung from our waists. Even Granny could see they were made us look like dumpy items of furnishing. But there was no question of us not wearing them.

'Mrs Addles may not be the most skilled of dressmakers, but she's a good woman at heart and terribly in need. She'll be very proud to know her handiwork's going to be seen by the bishop.'

On the evening of Confirmation, we assembled in the dining-room at the rectory with the ten other candidates. For the seven of us who were female, Granny brought down from the bottom drawer in her bedroom (where she kept old baby clothes for young mothers in need, and sticking plasters for minor injuries) the large white muslin squares which we were to wear.

'They look like nappies,' Mary whispered.

They smelled faintly of camphor.

With the help of one of the verger's wives, Granny tied

the squares to our heads with tapes that went round the backs of our necks. Suddenly they no longer looked like nappies and we no longer looked like spotty schoolgirls. With a smooth white band across our foreheads and white folds falling down behind, we were all transformed. Even the girl with wide flat cheeks and bulging eyes like a terrified rabbit, seemed to have a new ethereal quality.

The five youths each got a dab of Brylcreem and a turn with the comb.

The actual ratifying and confirming was not as difficult as I'd expected. When the bishop laid his hands on my head, although there was no flash of divine light, I felt hopeful, as though from now on I could probably face anything.

The trouble was, I was always getting this feeling of confidence and it was forever letting me down.

SIXTEEN

Angel Voices Singing

A few months later, on a murky damp afternoon, Veritas was overcome with one of those impulsive whims to be on the move.

'Come along, Mary, come along, Ruth,' she said. 'We've got to go over and visit your Grandfather.'

'Now?' I said. 'It's awfully late.'

'Yes. Straightaway. He needs me to take him a surprise.'

She was already walking up the lane to the Greenfinch's farm to borrow their truck.

'So what's this surprise you've got for him?' I asked when, half an hour later, we drew up in the dark at the back of the rectory.

'You. *You're* the surprise. Now *sssh*, or it won't be.'

Instead of going in through the back door, she hustled us round the side of the house. We knew it well enough to feel our way. Then along beside the high yew hedge, over the low box hedge and into a flowerbed full of crackling honesty beneath Grandfather's study.

'Now sing!' Veritas ordered in a whisper.

'Sing what?'

'Anything. What about a Christmas carol?'

'Which one?'

'Doesn't matter. Just do it. Please.' She was begging us.

Mary and I were not good singers, unless we were crooning along with Mario Lanzo. But Veritas's urgent mood was compelling. We sang 'The First Noel', falteringly at first, gaining strength as we remembered the words.

By the time we got to the third verse, a crack of light appeared at the window. The wooden shutters inside were folded back. It was the district nurse in her neat navy blue cap and cardigan. Behind her we could see our grandfather propped up in a single bed against the bird cages.

'Is he ill?' I asked.

'Not really,' said Veritas. 'Just feeling old.'

He must have heard the bad singing for we saw him slowly raise a hand towards the window.

'Angel voices!' we heard him call. 'I can hear the angels. Am I in heaven already?'

The nurse signalled through the pane to Veritas to come in.

'I'm not sure how pleased he'll be to see me,' Veritas whispered. 'You better wait here.'

So Mary and I shuffled about on the noisy seedpods and continued with 'Hark the Herald Angels Sing', as much to humour Veritas as our grandfather.

She didn't stay with him long but she was smiling when she re-emerged.

'Now *wasn't* that fun?' she said as we drove home. 'Nurse Wicks says he really enjoyed it.'

Mary and I were frozen through with the tingle of incipient chilblains in our toes. But if that was the penalty to pay for a truce between father and daughter, then it was probably worth it.

'And what about Granny? How was she?' Mary asked.

'Yes, what did Granny say?'

'I didn't go to see Granny,' Veritas said rather huffily.

'Didn't you even tell her you were there?'

'She'll be all right. She's got Speranza staying. I heard them chatting in the drawingroom.'

'But didn't you even want to say hello to her?'

'You know it's better if I don't stir her up. I only make her cross.'

The next time we saw Grandfather, he was rather nearer to meeting the real angels of heaven. He'd been moved to the Cottage Hospital because Nurse Wicks said that, as much as she loved the rector, she couldn't cope any longer in amongst the bird cages. Veritas went to borrow our neighbour's truck again.

Mary said, 'I bet he's missing his creatures. I better bring him Doris to cheer him up.' Doris was her favourite hen. 'And this time I think we should come in and see him properly. It's very humiliating having to wait outside.'

Veritas agreed, though persuaded her to bring a mouse

rather than a hen. This was just as well for, even without knowing about tiny Ernest Hemmingway tucked into Mary's gaberdine pocket, the nurses were hostile. The bishop of the diocese had already been in and stirred things up by demanding that the rector have a room of his own. The Cottage Hospital only had six rooms altogether.

We were bustled down a corridor.

'We put the reverend gentleman in here,' one of the nurses hissed, letting Mary and Veritas in. 'But the little girl must wait outside.'

'She's come to see her grandfather.'

'No children on the wards.'

'She's quite old enough. She's just very short for her age,' Veritas said.

'It's against the rules. And he can't talk. He's had a stroke. It might upset her.'

'Nonsense,' said Veritas firmly, pushing me through the door too. 'I've known him all my life. He never upsets people.'

'But he won't be able to say anything sensible,' the other nurse insisted.

Since Grandfather often talked in incomprehensible riddles, it seemed immaterial whether he would be talking today or not.

He lay alone in the small bright room, looking huge and magnificent on the bed. His white hospital gown was draped round him like a newly starched surplice. He was as still as one of the marble monuments in the side chapel at St Augustine's.

'Hello Father,' said Veritas. 'It's me, Vee, and I've brought my girls.'

'He can't recognise anyone. He doesn't know who you are,' said the nurse lurking in the doorway. But he knew we were there. He raised both arms in a silent greeting.

Mary took out Ernest, the brown mouse, and put it in the palm of Grandfather's hand. He smiled. He let it scamper up his arm, across his chest and down into the other hand. Then it clambered in and out between his open fingers as though on a miniature climbing frame. He seemed to be watching it though it was hard to tell for certain.

When Ernest left a small black dropping on the spotless counterpane, the nurses suddenly noticed what was going on. They darted forward, told us visiting time was over and made as much fuss about needing to change the bedding, as if a pet elephant had been let loose.

Grandfather lifted Ernest to his lips and gave it a gentle kiss. The mouse's soft whiskers brushed against the white stubble on Grandfather's chin. He raised his right hand and made the sign of the cross over us. I could almost feel it touching me with its illuminating power. This time, it was much more than a blessing. It was a farewell too.

Veritas sniffed and blew her nose. But there seemed to me no need to feel sad. Dying was obviously nothing to be afraid of.

'Of *course* she should cry if she wants to,' Mary

reprimanded me. 'He *is* her father after all.'

He died a few days later, was buried, and if his teaching of the scriptures was to be believed, immediately ascended to heaven to rejoin the parents who'd left him an orphan at the age of eight.

I said, 'I just hope they recognise him.'

If his own personal and non-scriptural views were to be believed, he also met again his favourite hunter who'd died in an accident, his beloved goats, kinkajous, and innumerable flights of canaries.

The bishop was no more compassionate than the nurses had been. Granny had to be out of the rectory immediately after the funeral was over. She'd lived and gardened there for thirty-five years. Now, she had no rights to remain. However much she was loved and admired by the parish, the bishop could make no exceptions. She had to make room for the next incumbent.

'She better come and live with us, hadn't she?' I suggested. It seemed the obvious solution.

'No, out of the question,' Veritas said quickly.

'Why not?'

Veritas could hardly make the excuse that there was no room. She didn't. She just said, 'You know very well why Granny shouldn't move in with us. Because it just wouldn't work. We'd all be too close. We'd get on top of each other. And anyway, I'm sure she doesn't even want to.'

Perhaps Veritas *did* understand her mother better than I did. Granny was busy making her own plans, without the help of any of her daughters, though they clucked to each other by letter, post card and telegram.

Granny had been offered, by a land-owner in her parish, the kennelman's flat on one of his farms. She accepted it and moved in without even consulting any of her daughters.

'Perhaps *you'd* better go and stay with her, Ruth, just for a couple of days,' Veritas suggested. 'It'd help her settle to have a familiar face. She always seems to feel better if you're around.'

Since I'd missed so much schooling when I'd been ill, Veritas didn't seem to think it mattered two hoots if I missed some more. For once, I agreed with her. Granny's immediate happiness was far more important than learning about the Wars of the Gauls.

All her adult life Granny had lived in Church of England rectories which may have been cold and unplumbed but had always had at least six bedrooms and five reception rooms. The former kennelman's flat was above some stables, right on the farmyard. For the first time in her life, Granny had no garden and only two cramped rooms. How on earth would she cope? How would she fit in all her furniture and pictures and books?

'Oh darling, I've given most of that stuff away,' she said breezily. 'You can't take them with you. There'll be treasure enough in heaven, and probably some nice bits of furniture too.'

Poor Jonq and Pol also had to get used to the lack of freedom. Every time the bull in its stall began bellowing, they cowered and whimpered in a corner of the poky bedroom. But Granny didn't complain about her altered circumstances.

'It's refreshing to have a change of scene,' she said, casting her short-sighted glance round the bleak flat. 'Without that herbaceous border to see to, I'm going to have all the more time for knitting. I'll be able to finish off the sleeves of your school jersey.'

She didn't shed a single tear over the loss of her husband. Had she developed a heart of stone?

'You don't need to cry on the outside, Ruth,' she said, 'for the Lord can see right into your heart. He knows how much a person is grieving.'

So, with her head held high and her blue felt hat pinned firmly in place, she faced widowhood with good grace.

Rejoice Evermore, and Pray without Ceasing, was engraved on her old silver pin-box. It was also written on her heart.

Nonetheless, Speranza, Charité, and Thrift went on worrying about her. Veritas, however, had quite other things on her mind, though she wasn't to know that widowhood was speeding her way too.

SEVENTEEN

Angel Voices Weeping

We'd seen Grandfather doing it. But it'd seemed less a case of dying than of fading. A natural, graceful ending to a splendid life. Certainly nothing to be sad about.

But when, one cold foggy morning only a few months later, our father died, it felt completely unexpected. It was too abrupt. I wasn't ready for it. There'd been no preparation for something so shocking.

I thought, fathers don't die!

But then, pretty little girls who wore frilly petticoats weren't supposed to die either. Yet Vivien had.

It was all right for her. She'd no responsibilities. Fathers did. They're meant to be there, if not forever, at least until their children had grown up and could cope with life. None of us had grown up, not even Mary. She was fifteen. Our little sister, Felicity the baby baby, was two. So how could he do this to her?

He'd been ill for a fortnight. And bronchitis was a serious illness, but no worse than any of the infections I'd had to put up with, and definitely not severe enough to expect it to make a person die.

I felt it was all quite unreal, like a dream we'd all wake up from, until Mary told me how she'd known that he was going to die for months and months.

I said I didn't know how she thought *she* knew, if even the doctors hadn't known.

She said, 'Father knew too. He's always known.'

I said, 'Don't be stupid. If he'd known, he'd have told us. And he hasn't finished writing his play yet. About Her Majesty's Foot Guards. He said he'd definitely got to finish it before he did anything else.'

Mary said, 'He's been waiting for it to happen ever since he was a young man, ever since the First World War when all his friends got killed.'

I still didn't believe her. How could being a soldier in a war when you were sixteen years old make you die from infected lungs nearly forty years later?

Of course, Mary didn't know the answer to that.

She, Alfred George, Blanche, Felicity and I gathered in the sullen dawn light in our parents' room, helpless as a litter of wet kittens to face this unforeseen calamity. Mary clung for comfort to her latest acquisition, a floppy puppy she'd rescued from the knacker's van.

As a confirmed person, surely I *ought* to be able to face anything? But not even loving and losing Vivien had warned me how fragile everyone's grasp on life really was.

The gaping hole was right here in the middle of our

family. Being so close to it, I saw that the aftermath of a death entailed more than weeping and wailing. There was so much paperwork. It had to be started right away, and each stage completed in the right order. First the doctor's declaration of death, then the post-mortem investigation to see what he'd actually died of. Nobody said anything about it being the First World War that had killed him.

Then came the issuing of the death certificate (which said he'd had pneumonia) and taking it to the Registrar's Office to register the death. Then receiving another form authorising legal burial. Then visiting the vicar. Then contacting the undertakers and finding out when they'd have a vacancy.

'A vacancy?' I said crossly. 'What do they mean? Are people supposed to make an appointment in advance so they don't all die at once?'

It seemed that every year, straight after Christmas and throughout the month of January, there was always a waiting list for funerals. It was the period of the year when the most people died, specially of pneumonia. And with the ground frozen solid, the grave-diggers' job was harder and took longer so the queue got longer.

Veritas dressed in her Sunday best, not one of the gaudy dresses made from Utility curtain fabric, but a sombre brown wool frock passed on by Aunt Charité. She set her hair in bobbi-pins, dabbed on a touch of face-powder, and sent a message to Granny telling her to come at once. Meanwhile, she set off to see to the awesome administration of death.

Granny turned up within an hour of the summons. No bottled plums, no eggs, no half-finished knitting, not even Jonq and Pol. Just her, in her felt hat (the black), her tweedy coat and skirt, her pearl necklace and her silent comfort.

She gave us each a kiss, then stirred up the grey embers in the bedroom grate until they jumped into life. She threw in a bundle of dry kindling. She built up a dancing fire. She pulled chairs round it. She didn't offer to play Spillikins or read aloud, or say prayers, or do anything to distract us. She did nothing but be reassuringly there, legs firmly planted on the rug, corsets creaking, hands ready to caress if needed, an old presence in a new loss.

'I was a child,' she said eventually, 'when *my* father died. Not as young as Felicity or Blanche, of course. I was Ruth's age.'

I knew about Grandfather's mother dying, then his father, leaving him orphaned by the age of eight, along with his ten siblings. But Granny's father too?

Then I remembered some of the agonised entries in the private penny notebooks. The longing and the missing. She never actually told me that it had been about her father. And I hadn't thought to ask.

'*On Sunday, in church,*' she'd written, '*I do so love looking out of the window opposite me in church. Though I do wonder if it's wrong and if I should stop. But the fields and distance and then the open sky are so lovely. And often there's a gleam of extra bright light which makes me think of Heaven.*

There was just such a gleam this morning and it looked as

though a little crack had got loosened so that some of the light from Heaven was getting through and then it made me think of him, my own darling. How I do miss him!'

She had been writing with such passion. No wonder I'd been confused over who or what she was missing. How could I have misunderstood? Then I saw Mary tightly hugging her doggy companion, burying her face in its ears, speaking to it as though to her one true friend. Perhaps, for some people, love for an animal could be as profound as love for another human. Certainly, that is what our Grandfather had believed.

'Oh what I would give to have him back,' Granny as a girl had written a whole long year after her father's death. *'How I do long for him, my own darling. I do wonder what he's doing. I wonder if he keeps Sunday separate, if he goes and sings specially beautiful hymns to Jesus? I wonder if his face looks the same? Oh how I do want him back. But that's wrong of me because he was so ill and Jesus wanted him.*

And how could she have experienced such loss, such grief, and not died of sadness herself, as I felt that I now would? How could we five children possibly manage to survive the rest of our lives without a father? Even though he'd never actually done much looking-after of us, his presence had always been there, blowing kisses to our mother, smiling benignly at us as we romped. Even when he sat hunched over his books, clearly not wanting to join in with the chattering of his children, he'd been there in a solid background way.

And now he wasn't. Death was the total severing of communication. He was quite out of our reach. And he'd had no right to have done this.

'You'll always miss him, of course,' Granny said quietly. 'All your lives, till you're quite old. You'll always remember how much you loved him. Put another log on the fire will you, Alfred George, there's a dear.'

We snuggled round Granny and her fire. 'And you'll all have to be even more helpful to your dear mother, won't you? Even you little ones are going to have to lend a hand, because it's not going to be easy. Things have never been easy for her. Of course, I'll do all I can to help too.'

Now that he was no longer here, Granny's anger at her most improvident son-in-law was also buried. She could find only positive memories of him.

'Such an *interesting* man,' she said, piling on the praise. 'Such a varied life he led. Such splendid work during the war. And such travels. He saw more of the world than I ever have. You'll remember him forever. In fact, the older you grow, the *more* you will remember his many wonderful qualities.'

'But he's *gone*,' I cried. It was no good her going on about what a wonderful person he'd once been in the past. I needed him to go on being a person, wonderful or otherwise, now, in the present, and into the future. 'We'll never ever see him again,' I wept.

'Not in this life, but in the life hereafter you will.'

Should I remind her that my father, unlike hers, had

been an agnostic? He had not believed in any god, nor in any afterlife. So, though Granny might expect to meet *her* father in heaven, there was no chance of me meeting up with mine.

I said, 'You *know* you can't get into heaven unless you're a confessing sinner, a repentant Christian. And he wasn't either of those.'

'Why, Ruth my dear, your father was a good, honest, generous man. And our Lord is a loving god. There will be no exclusions from heaven. Of that I'm sure.'

I wanted to believe her. But I suspected that, should my father unexpectedly find himself admitted through to the other side of those tall pearly gates free to wander forever in the gardens of Paradise, he'd be astonished. It'd be contrary to everything he'd anticipated. I could see exactly his expression of astonishment, with his eyebrows raised, his quizzical look, his monocole in one eye slipping out as he gave that short laugh that went, 'Ha!'

For a moment, it was almost as though I was there too, laughing at the joke of a non-believer finding himself arriving in heaven. I felt relief and laughed out loud too.

No. I wasn't with him. It was just a memory. If I wanted to see him again, I could only live in hope that he'd been wrong and that Granny was right, or that my father had had a change of heart at the last moment and become a repentant believer.

Then I had another hope. If I managed to live as righteous a life as my grandmother, might there be enough faith for both my father and me? Then, like Saint Christopher carrying the Christ child across the turbulant river, would my double-strength see us both into heaven?

Within a week of our father's burial, when Veritas and the five of us were still dopey with shock, and not able to see beyond the dark pit into which we'd all tumbled, Granny was already planning for the future. Hers and ours. She was making expansive and expensive arrangements. She was going to come and live permamently near us. Not near Thrift, Charité, or Speranza. Certainly not next door to any of her sons and their wives, but alongside the thoughtless, demanding and tearaway daughter with whom she'd had so many arguments.

In my view, there could be nothing more wonderful – apart from our father's immediate resurrection – than to have our Granny nearby. The twelve-mile bike ride was too long.

'But why's she choosing us rather than any of the others?' I wondered. Was it out of pity? I didn't want to be pitied, certainly not by my grandmother.

Granny came over with a land surveyor to view the only property available in the hamlet. On the edge of the field next door to our farmhouse stood a derelict building which had once contained three hundred hens. There'd been an outbreak of fowl pest. The birds had been destroyed. The hen-house hadn't been used since.

'I've always intended to move near to Veritas,' she said firmly. 'It's just been a matter of choosing the right moment.'

'So have they made it up d'you suppose?' I asked Mary.

She didn't think so. 'They'll probably go on annoying each other just the same as ever. It's what mothers and daughters are for. As long as we don't let ourselves get involved, it'll be all right.'

Granny had been born into a grand country mansion, yet she was intending to end her days in a disused hen farm. It was an ugly brick building, though Granny insisted the land around would make a wonderful garden.

'We'll soon have it looking pretty and cosy,' she said with the same confidence that Veritas showed about any impossible task. 'And I can already see exactly where I'll have my new herbaceous borders. And perhaps a water garden. I've always wanted to have a go at water lilies.'

When the labourers started work, one end of the rotten roof collapsed into a dusty heap of lathes and rubble. Only the walls of the hovel on which the hen-shed had been built were left standing.

'It was *never* my idea she should try and live so close,' snapped Veritas. 'She's only doing it to annoy me when she knows I'm not fit to fight back. I knew all along it wouldn't work out.'

'It's only the building that hasn't worked,' I pointed out reasonably. 'It's not the living here that hasn't worked.'

'Never mind,' said Granny. 'The Lord will send a solution in His own good time. I'm sure of it.'

'Youth can come and thtay in our houth and thleep in

my woom,' Blanche offered, flicking her auburn curls. 'You can hath *my* bed.'

'Mine too,' said Felicity solemnly. Whatever big sister Blanche did, she wanted to do too.

So Granny moved in with us. Since it was Blanche and Felicity who'd invited her, Alfred George who gave up his bed for her, Mary and I who put flowers in a vase on the dressing-table, there was no way Veritas could object.

Meanwhile, Granny's other daughters, who'd married sensible men with real jobs and regular incomes, had a whip-round and collected just enough money to re-build on the foundations of the fallen hen-house. It was to be a modest cottage with a large garden.

'It's very generous of them, isn't it?' I said.

Veritas didn't think so. 'They're only doing it for one reason. To make quite sure she doesn't move near them and meddle in their lives.'

But Granny had little time for interfering in Veritas's life. All day, every day, she was over in her muddy plot. She wore her galoshes and raffia garden hat, not to garden but to watch and supervise the progress of the future home. Every day, after school, Mary and I joined her to see how it was coming along.

'You may bury something in there, darlings, if you wish,' Granny said, as the builders stomped around with their barrow-loads of cement. 'There's still time.'

'How d'you mean?'

'Inside the walls. Right at the bottom. Before they re-do

the brickwork. I well remember when my dear father had the new coach-house put up, he let us hide our time-capsule.'

'Your what?'

'My sisters and I chose something of the present, as it was then, to leave behind so that people of the future would have a bit of our past to discover. Father gave us a lead-lined document case. I put in the *Illustrated London News*. Mother was so annoyed for she had not finished reading it. It's probably still there.'

We had no lead document case. But we found a sturdy shortbread tin with a tight fitting lid.

There were so many things I wanted to choose. If only I had Granny's penny books, I'd have put those as a memory for the future. But I had no idea where they were, perhaps already buried in some rubbish tip.

There wasn't time to start searching through the two tea-chests of Granny's remaining possessions stacked in our hall. The workmen had their next hodload of bricks ready. They took a patient ciggy-break while we finished packing our tin.

I put in the previous week's copy of *The Weekly Express* and *County Tribune*, hardly the same as the *Illustrated London News* of the 1890s, but at least it'd give future people a few ideas about our corner of southern England, and last year's cutting from *The Times*, already yellowing, describing our Grandfather's magnificent funeral, and the small newspaper announcement of our father's death. Also an unsuccessful sonnet I'd written while sitting beside our father's grave about black ravens in a cemetery.

My contribution to the tin was, I realised, all words in one form or another. So I added a blurry snap of Mary and me on the beach last summer.

Mary's contribution was much more interesting, a tail feather from her White Frizzle Bantam, a watercolour of her goat, and our 78 record of 'Love Me Honey, Baby Do'.

'You can't get rid of that!' I said.

'But it doesn't play properly. It's cracked. Maybe by the time someone finds it, they'll have invented a way to mend broken records.'

Alfred George, with Blanche and Felicity trailing along behind, came over to Granny's plot to see what we were up to. Blanche peered into the tin.

'Tha's no good!' she said. 'There'th no bithcuiths inthide. Tho there'th nothing for them to eat!'

We added a tin of Spam to the collection to sustain the diggers of the future. Then Alfred George put in a length of string with a special magic knot in it, and Felicity dropped in her favourite pebble with a hole in the middle.

'Bye bye my stone. See you again nover day,' she said as she watched Mary and me seal the tin with brown Butterfly tape.

Our ceremony wasn't only about burying bits of the present for the benefit of the future. It was also about Mary and me burying our childhood for the good of our siblings.

We had to leave behind girlhood. We'd promised Veritas we'd do our best to help bring up the younger ones. Promises were useless if you didn't try to keep them. Before we could help them grow up, we had to grow up.

I knew it'd begun happening to Mary. I definitely saw the builder's apprentice (fifteen, just left school, not yet shaving), wink at her as we shovelled rubble in on top of our tin.

And I was almost sure I saw Mary return his wink.

A barely perceptible signal of mutual recognition. No more than a faint blink. But a sister as astute as me notices everything, even the subtlest sign of love's blossoming.

EPILOGUE

The Happy Ever After

There were no more extensions to childhood. Mary and I began to venture beyond the family circle. We met other people we weren't related to. Sometimes we fell in love with them. We flapped our wings and we flew, just as Granny, such a long time ago, fell in love and flapped and flew from her family.

The little ones grew up too, though it took them a bit longer because they had further to go. One by one, we all of us fell in love; first Mary, then me, then our brother and eventually our two little sisters. And especially Veritas. That was the biggest surprise.

She'd been so very much in love with our father that we thought she would never be able to love another. We were wrong. Her enthusiasm and joy for life couldn't let her grieve for ever. She was like a young girl again, always managing to fall for the most unsuitable men. We were constantly having to rescue her.

'Not again? That really is the limit!' said Mary on one of

the occasions we'd rescued our dizzy mother from a devious schemer who mistook her for a rich and fascinating widow.

Fascinating, perhaps. Rich? No way.

As for Granny Ruth, she stayed on just where she was, in the poky cottage built on top of a disused hen-farm, next door to a rambling farmhouse that no longer had any of her own descendants living in it. I went to see her when I could. She kept the lumpy camp-bed always made up, in readiness for whoever who might need it.

She gardened in her yellow raffia hat, went to church in her blue felt hat, and wore her brown felt hat when receiving calls from the Women's Institute or bishop's wives. Jonq and Pol died. She didn't replace them. Instead, she took care of our pets when we couldn't fit them into our new bedsits, or when we went overseas.

One Sunday afternoon, I decided to take my current young man to visit her. I wanted to find out what she thought. I told him, 'It's a mystery trip.'

We left from Victoria Station. Then we walked from the railway halt, along the sunken lanes I knew so well, past the churchyard where my father was buried, past the Hare's and the Goldfinch's farms, past the sprawling house where I used to live.

We reached the cottage gate. We went up the path of the garden which would go on looking new for at least another decade.

'Hello, Granny. We just happened to be passing,' I lied. I

don't think my casual attitude was entirely convincing.

Granny prepared the usual tea as though she'd been expecting me. Bread that was only slightly stale. Shortbread biscuits that were only slightly soggy. She fetched an unopened jar of jam from the garden room.

'Perfectly fresh!' she declared. And indeed the firm blue mould crusting the surface proved it hadn't been opened until that day. I took a peek at the label.

'*Raspberry*', it said. '*July 1959*.'

Her writing had been firmer and steadier then. I glanced over the tea-pot to see if my companion knew how to cope with mould on jam. He did. Scrape it off surreptitiously. Put on side of tea-plate. Say nothing.

'Now then, young man,' said Granny when we'd finished. 'Perhaps you'd just sit there and admire the view for a few moments. I have a few things I wish to show my grand-daughter. And I may not see her again. I *am* eighty-four, you know.'

I followed her to her bedroom.

'And eighty-five next birthday,' she added, as though reminding herself how to count.

She walked slowly, touching the walls for balance, occasionally clutching at a chair-back for support. There was a creaking. Was it her pink corsets or the worn-out bones of her ancient joints? She used to be so tall. I remembered that day the war ended, how I'd had to crane my head right back to see her face way up against the clouds. Since then, I'd been growing. She'd definitely been shrinking.

'Now darling, what d'you want? I really do need to get it sorted out so there'll be no fuss. You've never mentioned anything so I simply don't know.'

I was startled. Was she giving away her possessions before she was even dead? It felt like looting even to think of choosing something to take away.

'I don't want anything, Granny, really I don't,' I said. Once, long ago, I'd wanted her penny books. But I'd started to write my own Private Journal and discovered it was the writing of it that was important, not the owning.

'Come along, don't dilly-dally. I'm sure you have your eye on something? Your Aunt Speranza wants the diamonds, or what's left of them. Thrift always asked for the pearls. Charité's after the fox-furs, though I can't think why. They're completely moth-eaten. And your own mother, well she's already had her share. She needed it, didn't she, when she was on such hard times? But I've put a few books aside that I know she'll be pleased to see again. And young Faith wants the Noah's Ark. So there must be *something* for you?'

Yes. I wanted the paradise part of my childhood back. I wanted to walk round the walled kitchen garden at St Augustine's rectory. I wanted to lead this young man between the box-hedged paths and show him the medlar tree, the peaches, pears, plums, the quince tree, mulberries, raspberries, loganberries, the figs, currants, red and white, the black grapes dangling from the vine in the greenhouse.

Granny pulled open the top drawer of the chest. She rootled around amongst lisle stockings, kid gloves, ivory-backed hair-brushes. She found a silver thimble, the golden cuttings of each of her babies' hair.

'No. That's not it,' she mumbled. 'Somewhere here.'

From under the clutter, she pulled out a folded tissue packet. She pushed it into my hands.

'There you are, darling.'

I unfolded brittle paper. I thought at first she was offering me a delicate hanky. But no, it was an antique baby's bonnet, hand-sewn from cotton and lace, with satin ribbons to tie under the chin.

'My first son's. Falcon. What a little charmer he was. And that's what I'd like you to have, Ruth, even if you won't take anything else.'

'I'm not – you know – Granny, honest.' I thought she thought I must be pregnant.

'I'm sure you're not, dear. Of course you're not.'

'If it was Uncle Falcon's, shouldn't one of his children have it?'

'Definitely not. They're not interested in old-fashioned things. Now, we better get back to that young lad before he gets tired of the view and wanders off. You don't want to lose him, do you?'

I guessed the lacy bonnet was a sign that she approved of the man. I shoved it into my skirt pocket. Too soon to show it to him. I hadn't made up my mind about him yet (even if my Granny had). He was going to West Africa for two years. If I wanted him, I'd have to go too.

Granny kissed the young man on the cheek as well as

shaking his hand. That was another good sign. But it was a wrench saying goodbye and leaving her all on her own in her doorway.

'Gracious me, darling! You don't need to go worrying about that,' she said. 'You've got to get on with your life. I've got to get on with mine. I've *such* a lot to see to. There's all those hyacinths to be potted up. The agapanthus needs attention. And the wallflowers to bed in.'

Eighty-four and still planting for the future.

She pointed out her last year's triumph with the camelia, her failure with the gardenia.

'Nipped by Jack Frost. Never mind, I'll try again next spring. Now, Ruth, you won't forget to take the plums this time, will you?'

We set off to walk back to the railway halt clutching our leaky Kilner jar of bottled plums, some jam with blue mould, but no eggs. The last train had gone. So we had to hitch back to London.

'She's a dear old dear, isn't she?' said the young man whose name was Harry.

'Yes.'

'She seems very fond of you.'

'Yes. Some people are. Only very special people, that is.'

He got the hint. He said he wanted to be one of the very special people who loved me. He asked me to stay with him for the rest of my life. I agreed. We married.

In Death's Dark Vale

We had a little girl called Merrily who wore the old lace bonnet. We lived in West Africa in a house with wattle walls and a corrugated iron roof. All around was inpenetrable green rain forest. There were vultures circling in the sky, and red-necked lizards in the compound.

I had another baby, Peregrine. He too wore his great grandmother's lace bonnet and, because it was so hot, not much else.

But then, there was fighting and turbulence between the tribes. 'Political instability,' the Foreign Office called it.

'Actually,' said Harry solemnly, 'this is civil war. And it's growing more dangerous.' He decided that even staying within our compound was no longer safe. He said, 'You must leave.'

I'd promised to stay with him for ever. But I agreed to go. Not because I was afraid for myself, but because I was afraid for our babies.

I travelled back to England and took crummy lodgings

while I decided what to do next. Perhaps Granny would let us stay in her garden room, as she had done in the past.

On our second day back in England, I was bathing my two tots in the chipped enamel sink when the landlady from downstairs came up.

'There's someone for you, love,' she said. 'On the telephone.'

'Thanks,' I said.

'Oooh, aren't they sweet,' she said of my children, pink and white and plump as marshmallows. Steamy tropical heat and a daily diet of fou-fou and yams hadn't harmed them.

'Ever such a posh voice,' said the landlady. 'Says it's an emergency. So she's holding on. I'll mind your bairns while you pop down.'

So far, only two people in the world, apart from Harry, knew where I was – Veritas and Mary. I guessed which one it must be. But what emergency could there be that was worse than the turmoil of the country I'd just returned from?

'Ruthie! Darling!' sang the distant voice on the telephone. It was Veritas of course. 'Haven't got long. We're at the airport. We're just off to Venice. Flying Air Italia!'

'We?' Who was 'we' this time?

And flying to Venice? Since when did that count as an emergency?

'Oh,' I said. 'That's good.'

'Venezia. La Serenissima! Aaah,' she sighed. 'Anything you want me to bring back?' Without waiting for a reply, she went on, 'Fettucine! That's what. Hand-made. I can hardly wait to be there. So can you do something, please, Ruthie, while I'm away? Will you try and pop down to see your Granny?'

'Yes. Actually I was intending to go as soon as I can.' I hadn't yet worked out how. I had no car. My only available money was all in kobo, and little coins with holes in the middle like the pebbles my younger sister liked as a child. 'Granny hasn't met my new baby yet.'

Nor, come to that, had Veritas. But she wasn't so interested in babies.

'I know it's difficult for you, Ruth, when you've only just got back from China or wherever it was you've been hiding.'

'Working. And it was West Africa.'

'Quite. But it'd be fun for you and you know how much you always cheer her up. Apparantly she's had a tiny weeny stroke. So the poor old girl's not feeling very well.'

'Of course I'll go. And I'll get Merrily to make her a get-well card.'

She laughed. 'You can hardly wish someone to get well from being old! It's usually irreversible!'

'Mum, do you think you could—?' I began. I was going to say, do you think you could lend me some money, just to see me through the next couple of weeks? But she'd run out of time.

'Ooh, that's our flight number. Just being called. Better go. Byee!'

'Bye then. Hope you have a wonderful time,' I managed to say. But the line was already purring so I don't expect she heard.

I tried to think generous thoughts. I'd come back to Britain after about nearly two years away and she didn't even have time to talk to me on the phone. I climbed the stairs to my rooms feeling weary. I hoped it wasn't malaria. With any luck, it was only jet-lag.

Merrily made five get-well cards with a mess of glue and cut-up paper scraps. But before the glue was even dry, the cards were obsolete. My landlady came puffing up the stairs again and handed me a brown manila enevelope.

'Telegram! You are a busy girl!' she said. 'Much in demand!'

It was from my sister Mary.

DID YOU KNOW STOP GRANNY DIED THURSDAY STOP CANT CONTACT MUM STOP PLEASE GO TO FUNERAL STOP TAKE FLOWERS AND LOVE FROM US STOP

I thought how peculiar it was that Veritas should have decided to go to Venice this very week. Had she known Granny was dying? Was new love more important than an old mother?

Yes, that's exactly what she'd have said. Love is the most important thing in the world. Love is stronger than mountains.

I filled the babies' bottles with milk. Merrily was three, but she still liked a bottle to be like her brother. I made cheese sandwiches. I asked to borrow a fiver from my long-suffering landlady.

'Well really! I don't know what you been up to in foreign parts. But this isn't normal round here,' she said, clicking her tongue with disapproval. 'Usually, it's my tenants as give the money to me, not me handing it out to them.'

But when I said I had to get to my grandmother's funeral, she lent me a tenner instead. 'Providing you won't be trying this trick on every week.'

I got my babies up from their nap. I told them, 'Wake up sleepy-heads. We're going on an adventure.'

'Where's our Papa?' said Merrily.

'Pa pa pa ba ba ba,' said Peregrine.

I said, 'He's still on his adventure. This one's going to be ours.'

Dust To Dust

Long after nightfall, when the tawny owls were already hooting in the trees, I was bumping the push-chair down the lane. I reached the gate. I pulled aside a tangled mat of couch grass. I had to shove hard to get the gate to open. I could feel dandelions underfoot. It must be a long time since she'd been well enough to potter out with her weeding hoe.

The key was in its place, on a string under the fuschia bush.

My cargo were lolling like drunken sailors.

'Up you come, sweetiepies.' I lifted them one by one and staggered with them indoors.

Merrily tried to wake herself for whatever excitement might be next. 'We there now? Is this the church with the singing?' Always on the look-out for fun. Rather like her grandmother Veritas.

'Not quite, sweetheart. This is my Granny's home,' I said. And what was going to happen to it? I supposed the uncles would sort it out.

'Granny?' she said hopefully.

'No, not *your* granny. She's in Italy. Remember, I told you? *My* granny. Your great granny.'

'Ah,' she murmured. 'Old lady. With old things.'

'That's the one. We'll spend the night here.'

She'd nodded off again.

I slid them both straight into Granny's high mahogony bed. The room smelled of composting leaves, and there were fresh cobwebs draped like a shroud over the sad feet of the crucifix on the wall beside her bed.

'So that's the first thing each morning that my eyes fall upon,' she used to say.

Even the damp felt friendly. Mildewed sheets and mustiness were part of any return. The only thing missing was the three-minute boiled egg and bread and butter fingers. I poked around in her larder, expecting to find a jar of jam with blue on top, or a punnet of strawberries with furry grey undersides like rabbit fluff. No. She must have been in hospital too long. Someone'd been in to tidy up. Just some evaporated milk — that'd do for the children's breakfast — and a tin of sardines so rusty it might even have been pre-war. It had no key.

Merrily muttered in her sleep as I climbed into the bed beside her.

'Only me,' I whispered. 'I used to sleep here sometimes, just like this, all in a row with your Aunty Mary and our Granny.'

Merrily snuggled up on one side, Peregrine on the other,

like snuffling piglets against the sow. They hadn't whined on the long journey, or complained that they didn't know where they were going. They had such trust. I hardly deserved it.

As I too fell asleep, I remembered I hadn't put a nappy on Merrily. Granny didn't like it when we wet her bed. Then I remembered. Where Granny was now, all wettings were eternally forgiven.

Next day, the sandy-headed young man standing stiffly in the church porch looked both a stranger, yet as familiar as someone from a dream. He had a freckled nose, similar to my own, and to little Peregrine's. Had we inherited that bumpy pumpkin from Granny? He was in dark blue uniform. From the way he was keeping watch, he could almost have been his own father. Keen-eyed, more like a hawk than a sea-bird, he gazed towards the lych-gate to see who might turn up next.

So Cousin Cormorant had joined the Royal Navy!

When he smiled, I saw that his broken front tooth had been fixed. What a pity. I'd always admired it. It reminded me of when we were young and how brave he'd been, falling against the iron railings by the well and hardly making any fuss at all. Was he still brave? Was he still annoying? Did he still like bossing people?

He came eagerly forward to greet me, almost running. 'Yes. It *is*! It's dear little cousin Ruth.'

For a moment I thought he was about to start teasing me, just as he always did when we were children. But no.

He looked genuinely pleased to see me. We definitely weren't here to rake over old tiffs. We were here to let the Lord make His face to shine upon us, out of respect for our grandmother.

'Hello, Cormorant,' I said.

He kissed me on both cheeks. 'It's really fanastic to see you again, Ruth.'

The sexton began fussing around in the porch.

'Not a very good time of year,' he said dismally. 'For funerals. So many people away at this time of year.' He popped back inside the church like a cuckoo into a wooden clock.

'Odd,' said Cormorant. 'When does he think *is* a good time? And I wonder if he says the same about weddings?'

We were the only grandchildren to turn up. All the rest of the cousins scattered to the four corners of the earth, working or studying.

I said, 'D'you remember, whenever she got a letter with a foreign stamp?'

'Yes, she'd make the postman sit and wait while she read it out loud.'

'Because she was so proud that she had friends and relations all over the world. Then she'd put the letter up on the kitchen dresser so we could admire it.'

'When he was in China, my father sent special jasmine tea.'

'I remember. That went on the dresser too. The stamps were amazing.'

So wasn't this more or less how she'd have wanted it? Everybody busy about the world. Nobody wasting their time over burying the dead.

My little daughter Merrily romped on the grassy mounds. Peregrine toddled backwards and forwards, using head-stones to keep his balance. Perhaps they thought this was the funeral, them playing, me and my cousin chatting under a yew tree? In the soft sunlight, it certainly didn't feel sad to be here.

'Nice sprogs,' Cormorant said, smiling.

'Thanks,' I said.

'But then, I always knew you'd have decent ones.'

'I don't know how you *could've* known that. I wasn't intending to have any at all. At least, not quite so soon.'

'You were always such a smashing little girl yourself, even when you were so ill.'

Was I? I always felt I was hopeless and lumpy.

He said, 'D'you remember when we used to stay with Granny and Grandfather?'

'Of course.'

'I liked it best when you and your sister were there too.'

Had he? Why had he never said so at the time? As I remembered it, he always found Mary and me as intensely irritating as we found him.

Perhaps I'd remembered wrong. Or he had.

'You used to call me a soppy cissy,' I said, laughing.

'How perfectly beastly of me. So uncivilised. I don't

remember that at all. I always thought you were just wonderful.'

Other parts of our memories were more similiar. The mulberry tree and its dark staining fruit, the dribbling noses of the two Pekinese, the shrill bark of Grandfather's terriers, and the brevity of his sermons.

What a pity I hadn't noticed what an easy-going person Cormorant was when we were younger. Or perhaps neither of us was then.

The sexton popped out of the west door again.

Cormorant said, 'Looks like he wants us to go in and get started.'

'But I thought we were waiting for Granny? The hearse, and all that.'

'No. The coffin's already inside.'

'Oh dear. I didn't realise.' But I should've. She always liked to be in good time for a service.

Merrily began jumping up and down. 'Bury it! Is the burying going to begin?'

'Soon,' I said. 'Prayers and singing first.'

Cormorant interrupted. 'Er actually, Ruth, no burial.'

I thought, What a shame. Granny liked burying things, mostly bulbs of course. She called it squirreling.

'Not my idea. The others, Father, the uncles and aunts, they all thought, since they couldn't make it today, it'd be best if she was cremated.'

'Cream ate it?' Merrily demanded. 'Wha's that? Can we have it too?'

'Sh, I'll explain later.'

Cormorant said, 'They'll have a big junket later on with everybody there and then she can go in the same er-, last er-, you know, last resting place as Grandfather.' He obviously didn't have the same fascination for talking about graves as I did.

'Death's never very convenient, is it?' he added with an embarrassed glance. 'Anyway, whatever they decide, I shan't be there. That's why I wanted to come today. I've been posted to Hong Kong. Leaving Thursday.'

'How long?'

'Three years.'

What a pity. He was going off just when we'd re-met.

'Maybe you'll have had some more nice babies by then,' he said.

'Maybe you will too?'

I gathered up my children and we went in.

Meg, the all-purpose maid, was here. And so was daft Amy, whom Granny had rescued from an existence of darkness in a back room. Good old Meg had thought to bring her from the Home. And a few people from the farming families in the hamlet. And two unidentifiable old ladies, perhaps from the Women's Institute, the organist, me and my two children, and my cousin. Little more than a dozen in all.

I smiled hello to Meg and Amy, though I wasn't sure they recognised me, and shuffled Merrily and Peregrine into a pew. Cousin Cormorant went marching slowly forward down the aisle, straight-backed, stiff as a tin sailor, arms like rods by his sides. When he reached the chancel steps, he gave a rapid reverent bow towards the altar, then another more slowly to our grandmother's coffin. It was all as solemn as if this was a state funeral for some monarch or minister, though there was no marching band to keep time to.

The organ groaned into life.

'We plough the fields and scatter, the good seed on the land.'

What a strange choice of hymn! Perhaps Cormorant thought it was her favourite? I'd always thought The Lord's my Shepherd was. Perhaps our Granny had had several favourite hymns just as she'd obviously been able to have several favourite grandchildren. In fact, perhaps each one of us had been her special favourite at some moment or another?

We sang, we prayed, we listened to a young vicar who hadn't even known her, say some good words before commending her spirit into the care of the Lord. This, in my opinion, was quite unnecsssary. She'd prayed every morning of her life. If God had been listening, He'd have noticed the recent silence and long since received her into His care.

Without ever going out to work, she'd still had a long active life, committed to filling other people's lives with love and flowers.

Where were all those people?

When it was my turn for a funeral, would there be so few present?

The prayer of commital was over. I glanced towards Cormorant. I saw tears begin to glint, to brim full, caught for a moment by his sandy red eyelashes, then spilling down his pink cheeks. A grown man, nearly thirty. Soon be middle-aged. But not so hard and old that he couldn't cry for his granny.

His tears initiated mine. Welling up and splashing down. On to the hymm book, on to the cross-stitch hassock on the floor. How many previous mourners had saturated that embroidered lamb?

Merrily tugged at my skirt. 'Mumma, mumma, why you crying now?'

Because there just hasn't been the right moment till now.

'Because my Granny died,' I sniffed. Merrily wasn't yet four so how could she understand the sweetness of grief? The memories and missing which ebb and flow and never go away altogether.

I whispered, 'And I'm crying because I know I'm going to miss her so much. I don't know what I'll do without her.' Even old and forgetful, she'd been there, holding on to the past which contained my childhood so that I could get on with living. Now I'd have to let it all go.

I remembered how Veritas had once told me that I owed my life to her for giving birth to me. Shortly after, Nurse Grim had told me I owed my life to the discoverer of penicillin. But I had firmly decided that I owed my life to

Granny. To my surprise, when I told her, thinking she'd be pleased, she'd said, 'We all owe our lives to God for His bounteous mercy. But since He doesn't give us very much time on earth, one might as well do the best with it one can.'

While I blew my nose, Merrily hummed lustily along with the final hymn. Then she whispered, 'Mumma, you can think of nice things about your Granny, then you won't be so sad.'

And suddenly I could hear the ringing tones of my Granny's voice calling me. 'Darling Ruth, do come out and look! The Lent lilies are so lovely today. Just a sea of gold.'

The coffin was carried out. Cormorant followed. Merrily said, 'Don't cry no more, Mumma. Your old lady Granny's not crying. She's dancing with the angels in the heaven.'

'How d'you know?'

'I just knowed it. I can see her.' Merrily waved her chubby hand up to the vaulted ceiling, shaped like the bottom of a boat. Carved oak angels appeared to be floating in a static dance among the woodwormed beams.

Merrily's right. No more grief. Granny's had a life, from start to finish. All wrapped up now. Time to rest. Time to dance.

So goodbye, Granny. God bless. Rejoice evermore.

As it was in the beginning, for ever and ever, Amen.

Read more from Rachel Anderson

Moving Times: Book One

BLOOM OF YOUTH

How was I to know that this rambling country Paradise couldn't last? They say we're in the bloom of youth. Ripe for transformation from uncouth savages to marriageable young ladies. But my sister says that out there is REAL LIFE. Bursting with Passion. Love. Fulfilment. We've got to find it.

For young Ruth the future beckons, rich with dreams. But this is the 1950s. There's no halfway between girlhood and womanhood. So where does a schoolgirl seek Life and Hope? Before it slips away, beyond reach?

Moving Times: Book Three

STRONGER THAN MOUNTAINS

Throughout the years that Veritas has spent trying to rear me, there's one essential truth she's always stuck to. 'Love is stronger than mountains.' My mother's name means truth. But can any of us trust her to tell the truth about our family?

As Ruth stands at the altar promising love to this young man till the end of life, under her breath she makes another vow: to set down everything of the past – the reality of a girlhood constantly touched by sadness, yet always profoundly secure.

Praise for the *Moving Times* trilogy:

'An appealing mixture of humour and poignancy.' *Books for Keeps*

'Funny, with a melancholy edge.' Philip Pullman, *Guardian*

'An evocative trilogy.' *Times Educational Supplement*

'Sad, funny, ironic, thoughtful and entertaining.' *School Librarian*

'An evocative picture of a girl growing up.' *Carousel*

'Anderson handles difficult situations with tact and humour and produces strong, believable characters.' *Glasgow Herald*

'The always reliable Rachel Anderson.' Linda Newberry, *TES*

'A past master of her craft.' *Publishers News*